# Tara Takes THE Stage

ALSO BY TAMSIN LANE

*Yael and the Party of the Year*

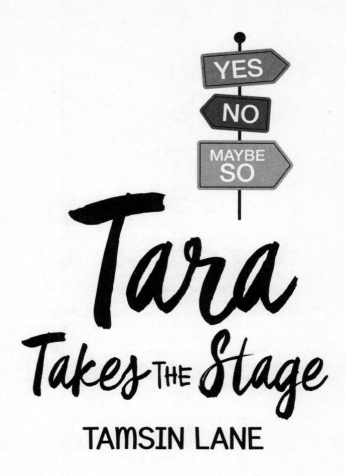

# Tara
## Takes the Stage

### TAMSIN LANE

**SIMON & SCHUSTER CANADA**
NEW YORK  LONDON  TORONTO  SYDNEY  NEW DELHI

SIMON & SCHUSTER CANADA

A Division of Simon & Schuster, Inc.

166 King Street East, Suite 300

Toronto, Ontario M5A 1J3

For information about special discounts for bulk purchases, please contact
Simon & Schuster Special Sales at 1-800-268-3216 or CustomerService@simonandschuster.ca.

Text by Joanne Levy

Book design by Alicia Mikles

The text for this book was set in Lomba.

Manufactured in the United States of America

0418 FFG

First Edition

2 4 6 8 10 9 7 5 3 1

Library and Archives Canada Cataloguing in Publication

Lane, Tamsin, author

Tara takes the stage / Tamsin Lane.

(Yes no maybe so)

Issued in print and electronic formats.

ISBN 978-1-5011-7568-8 (hardcover).—ISBN 978-1-5011-7609-8 (softcover).—
ISBN 978-1-5011-7611-1 (ebook)

I. Title.  PS8623.A5226T37 2018  jC813'.6  C2017-905584-4  C2017-905585-2

## How to read a
## Yes No Maybe So book

As you read you will come across a set of choices. Turn to the page shown and continue reading until your next set of choices. When you get to the end, you can start all over again!

# The Curtain Rises

"My hearrrrrrt can't choooooose . . . ," I belted out along with the music as I scooped a bunch of samosas out of the fryer with the long-handled basket. As always—when I made them—they were a perfect, delicious golden brown. I dumped them on the rack to cool and put another batch in the oil to cook.

My family's sweet shop—Mmmumbai—wouldn't open for another hour. I had cranked up the stereo while I cooked. My parents didn't mind, as long as it wasn't so loud that it "shook the rafters" of our apartment upstairs and I turned it down before the store opened. But by then I'd be long gone on my way to school.

Until my best friend, Yael Lewis, showed up to walk to school with me, I was on my own to cook and sing. I turned up the volume a little more and shimmied around the room.

"…I loooooked up aaaaand—*urgleaaaahhhh!*"

"Urgleaaaahhhh" isn't part of the song, but it *is* what you blurt out when you're singing at the top of your lungs, thinking you're alone, and you turn and there's someone standing right beside you. And that someone is smirking.

"Rohan!" I yelled. "You could warn a person!"

Rohan laughed, his eyes wrinkling at the corners. "I *did* try to warn you, Sitara; I called out your name six times!"

"Whatever," I said, smiling as I pictured what he'd seen. Whenever I sang, I felt strong and light at the same time. My voice became deeper and richer as I breathed through the notes, and the rest of my senses shut down as I soared along with the music.

I quickly turned back to the fryer to make sure the samosas didn't burn.

"You sounded good, though," he said. "You have a really nice voice."

I turned my head to look at him and lifted an eyebrow, waiting for the punch line, but he just smiled at me. Maybe it wasn't a joke, and he really meant it. I *did* have a great voice, one that would get me to Broadway someday, but *he'd* never mentioned it before. I realized I'd been staring at him a beat too long. "Uh, thanks," I said, turning back toward the fryer again. "So, what are you doing here?"

It wasn't strange that he was there; he worked part-time at the sweet shop and was practically a family member, he was there so much. Our mothers were best friends, and I'd known him forever. I used to see him at school, too, but it was different this year since he was now in ninth grade, which meant we weren't in the same building anymore. He only came over after school, when I was usually staying late for drama club. We hadn't seen each other much lately.

I peeked at him again; he looked taller than I remembered.

His shoulders moved as he shrugged. "Your mom texted me last night that she got a last-minute catering order for this morning. Since I have first period free, I can deliver it."

I pointed at the fryer. "I'll just finish with

these, then I'll go up front to pack it for you."

He nodded and grabbed one of the cooling samosas, juggling it from hand to hand. "Hot, hot, hot!" A second later he took a bite and made a face. "Ugh, this isn't one of the apple cinnamon ones."

I snorted. "I never said it was." My family was known for our untraditional twists on traditional Indian sweets. But we still offered some savory staples. "These are just regular potato and pea. The apple cinnamons are already out in the case. But, um, isn't that burning your tongue?"

He shrugged and took another bite. "Still good," he said as he chewed, steam escaping his open mouth.

"Weirdo," I said, and we both laughed.

Once I was done with the samosas, I went out to the front of the store where the big glass display cases were already filled with pastries and goodies for the day.

My parents baked almost everything very early (getting up in the middle of the night most days), but when they were done, they always took a short rest upstairs before the store opened, leaving a few things for me to make so I could earn some money.

While Rohan waited, eating his samosa, I looked at the computer to find the order that he would be delivering.

"Three dozen assorted," I said when I pulled up the invoice. With a nod, I printed it out and turned to grab one of the big saffron-colored pastry boxes.

As I was arranging the last of the maple syrup laddus (sort of like a doughnut hole but a billion times better) in the box, my parents came through the back of the shop. They were both carrying steaming mugs of chai.

"Good morning, Rohan," my father said. He came up to me and gave me a kiss on the crown of my head before he reached into the case for a jalebi, his favorite sweet.

"Is that the order for the bank meeting?" my mother asked, nodding toward the box in my hands.

"Yes," Rohan said. "I'll take it right over as soon as Sitara finishes packing it up."

I wrapped string around the box—heavy with its sugary load—to secure it before I taped the receipt on top. "There you go," I said, holding out the box toward him.

He stepped forward, and as he reached for the

box, the tips of his fingers brushed against mine. And then he didn't move away. My eyes darted up to his, wondering why he'd frozen in place, only to find he was staring at me. Not just *looking* and definitely not *glaring*. *Staring*.

So weird!

Then, as though it weren't weird AT ALL, he smiled, took the box, and exited while I stood there like a stage prop.

Mom sipped her tea and grinned at me over her mug. "What a nice boy," she said. Had she noticed what he'd done?

Mom was *always* talking about Rohan like that. "Oh, Rohan's so nice; oh, Rohan's so reliable; oh, Rohan is so good-looking and comes from such a nice family, blah, blah, blah."

He *was* nice and reliable and, I guess, good-looking, too, with his dark hair and cute smile. I'd never really thought about him that way. I'd never really thought about him before at all.

"There's Yael," my father said, breaking into my thoughts. He nodded toward the front window. Sure enough, my BFF was standing outside, waiting for me.

I waved at her and ran to the back to quickly wash my hands and grab my backpack for school.

As I returned to the front of the store, Dad handed me a small bag.

"Coconut laddus," he said as I took it.

"Her favorite," I said. "Thanks." And then I got up on my tiptoes and gave him a kiss on the cheek.

"Don't forget I have drama club after school today," I called out as I left.

As I walked toward Yael, I noticed her face was lit with excitement. Something was up. "What?" I asked right away because she obviously had news. "WHAT?"

She pulled a sheet of paper out of her pocket and unfolded it, holding it up for me to read.

It only took a second for me to scan what it said. She lowered the paper, and we looked at each other with wide eyes. Then we both screamed in excitement.

I looped my arm through hers, and we skipped toward school.

"We're off to see the wizard . . . !"

# The Costar

We got more than halfway to school before we grew tired of skipping and singing at the tops of our lungs (well, *I* was singing at the top of my lungs; Yael was just singing regular, but she doesn't love singing the way I do).

We had stopped and were laughing when some younger kid walked by us with a terrified look on his face.

"What, you've never seen *The Wizard of Oz* before?" I leaned over toward him and asked. "Because, because, because, because, BECAAAAAAAUSE!" I took a big inhale, but before I could finish, the kid shook his head and ran away from us. Yael and I laughed again.

When we had finally caught our breath, Yael looked at me sideways with a sly smile. "So, I guess this means you're *not* going to try out, huh?"

"Right," I said with a laugh. "Like you could stop me from trying out for *The Wizard of Oz*! I will be the best Dorothy EVAH!"

"I can't wait!" Yael said. "And of course we'll get to do this together."

She held up the flyer again and pointed at the bottom where it said they were also looking for set designers and techs.

"You're the best painter in our grade. You will make the most stunning, beautiful, Ozerific sets anyone has ever seen!"

She smiled and nodded enthusiastically. "Right?" But then she gave me a funny look and clutched her stomach. "Unless . . . ugh . . . unless I die of starvation first."

I just stared at her in confusion until her eyes darted pointedly down toward the bag in my hand.

I snorted. "Such drama! And here I thought *I* would be the one who'll win a Tony one day!" I said. She took a big bow, complete with a graceful flourish of her arm.

I shook my head at her as I handed her the bag of treats. My bestie didn't want to be famous like I did, but we liked to share the role of funny friend. It was just one of the things I loved about her.

I was crouched down, putting my backpack into my locker, when I sensed someone—and not a Yael-size someone—come to stand beside me.

I looked up and almost fell backward. It was Hiro Nakahara, captain of the lacrosse team, the school's best dancer, and the most popular boy. He also happened to be my crush since sixth grade. He'd been my partner for folk dancing in gym class and had told me I had great moves, which, coming from him, was a huge compliment.

So, there he was, right beside me. Looking at me. ME!

"Hey," he said.

*OMG, OMG, OMG!* whirled around in my head as I closed my locker and stood up, grateful that even though my legs suddenly felt wobbly like spaghetti (because he was *right there* and he was *smiling*—at *me*!), they worked. He was looking right into my eyes, so he *had* to be talking to me, but it took me a second to chill and croak out "Hey" back.

He didn't seem to notice how nervous I was and was still smiling when he said, "Did you hear about the auditions?"

Hiro and I were in drama club together, and, just like me, he was obsessed with all things theater. Of course he'd heard about Knot's Valley Little Theater's casting call.

I nodded.

"You're going to try out, right?"

I nodded again and then realized I probably needed to say something out loud, using actual words. *You're an actress,* I told myself. *Act like a cool person!*

"Yeah," I said with a one-shoulder shrug that I desperately hoped looked casual. "I mean, yeah for sure. For Dorothy, obvs."

"Awesome," he said, his grin widening. "I'm going to be the Scarecrow. I *was* going to be the Tin Man, but I think the Scarecrow has a bigger part."

"Good call," I said.

Then he said, "I look forward to being the Scarecrow to your Dorothy."

Gulp. He was looking at me, like, *really*

looking at me, and not just because I happened to be in front of him, but because he *wanted* to look at me. My heart thumped so hard it was very obvious I was not lacking that organ, nor was I made of tin.

I suddenly ran out of words, which *never* happens to me. Thankfully, Yael had my back. I'd forgotten she was even there but was so glad she was. "The Scarecrow is a really hard role—it's so physical."

Hiro smirked, showing off his dimple, and I reminded myself to blink. "That's one of the things I love about it," he said. And then he did this wobbly dance that made him look like he had no bones. A second later he began to sing, "If I only had a braaaaain . . ."

I glanced over at Yael, and I could see she was impressed too. I felt weirdly proud, even though he wasn't my boyfriend . . . yet.

Yael and I applauded right there in the hall-way. "Obviously, you're going to crush the audition," I said, and then realized I'd said "crush." Heat rushed to my cheeks.

He bumped his shoulder into mine. "You will too, Tara. Make sure you're at drama club after school so we can practice."

I nodded. "I wouldn't miss it!"

Just then the two-minute bell rang.

"Come on, I'll walk you to class," Hiro said, looping his arm through mine. I looked down at where we were joined and then back up to his face. Was this my real life? There's no place like . . . right here in the hallway with Hiro.

He tugged me down the hall when he began to sing in his clear voice: "Weeeeeee're off to see—"

"Hiro!" I said, planting my feet on the floor and stopping him.

He did an exaggerated wobble as though he were going to fall over but then caught himself at the last second—he was going to be the perfect Scarecrow. "Yeah?"

I nodded toward the other end of the hall. "Our class is *this* way."

Looking up and pointing his finger at his temple, he made a goofy face. "Oh, yeah!" he said with a wink, and then began to sing: "If I oooooonly had a brain!"

Then he spun me around, and we skipped to class. Halfway there, I glanced over my shoulder and mouthed to Yael: "Oh. Em. Gee!"

# Special Guest Appearance

"If only Dorothy got to kiss the Scarecrow," I said right before taking a bite of my carrot stick. It was lunchtime, and I was in the cafeteria sitting with Yael and our two other friends, Paloma and Gemma.

Yael rolled her eyes. "Dorothy is supposed to be a young girl. The Scarecrow's a grown-up."

Gemma wrinkled her nose. "That's gross."

Paloma only nodded in agreement since her mouth was full of sandwich, though she did it very exuberantly.

"Yes, but *my* Scarecrow will be the same age

as me. I bet if Judy Garland's Scarecrow had been her age and cute, with spiked-up black hair and gorgeous hazel eyes, she would have kissed him."

"That's not the point," Yael countered. "There's no kissing in TWOz." (TWOz—rhymes with "gauze"—was our code name for *The Wizard of Oz*.)

I opened my mouth to say *Too bad*, but before I got the chance, someone cleared their throat next to me.

I had a quarter of a second to hope it was Hiro before I looked over and saw Desmond Flynn.

"Hi, Des," Paloma said.

Paloma was in gaming club with Desmond and talked about him sometimes. She said he was a little shy but really smart, and if you put a controller in his hand, suddenly he wasn't so shy anymore. The way she went on about him, I thought she might have a crush on him, but she always denied it. I wouldn't blame her if she did, though, since he *was* kind of cute. Though with how quiet he was, he wasn't drama club material, that's for sure.

Yael asked, "What's up, Desmond?" because he was just sort of standing there, holding a tray as we looked at him.

He pointed at the empty chair beside me. "Do you mind if I sit here?"

"Nope, go ahead," I said. I was going to suggest I trade spots with Paloma so they could sit together, but when I glanced over, she shrugged, and I didn't want to embarrass her.

Desmond's tray clattered a little as he put it down. He usually sat with an assortment of gamers and theater tech kids. I looked around and found his regular table; all his friends were watching us.

Maybe he *was* into Paloma and had come over to sit with her. I looked at him, but he was smiling at *me*.

I returned his smile and then looked back at my friends. "So as I was saying," I continued. "He'll be the perfect Scarecrow, and then I guess Meg can be the Witch." Because there was no way Meg Hamilton was going to beat *me* out for the part of Dorothy. Not in a million years.

Desmond spoke up. "Are you talking about Knot's Valley Little Theater?"

I looked back at him and smiled. "Yeah. Are you trying out?"

This was a twist. Desmond Flynn onstage? The way he was shy and quiet made it seem like he'd be a good Cowardly Lion, except he wasn't putting on an act. Actors can't actually *be* cowardly and shy.

"Oh, no!" he said, "I'm hoping to work as a tech. I do lighting."

"Cool!" Yael leaned forward. "I want to do set design."

He nodded and took a sip of his chocolate milk.

"I'm going to be Dorothy," I announced.

"You'll be perfect as Dorothy," Desmond said quickly. "You have such a great voice."

"How do you know?" I blurted out—I didn't think he'd ever seen me perform—and then added, "And thanks," because it was nice for him to have said so.

"Because while you're onstage during drama club, I'm in the booth working the lights."

I'd never realized anyone other than the rest of drama club ever paid attention, but obviously there were other clubs I hadn't given much thought to, like film club, chess club, and I guess backstage lighting club.

I was about to say something when there was suddenly a lot of noise coming from the right side of the cafeteria: raised voices, but not a fight—happy voices.

"What is it?" Paloma asked.

"I don't know." I turned and craned my neck, and then when I still couldn't see over the crowd of students, I stood up. "Rohan?"

There he was, standing by the door, a bunch of kids (and even Mr. Stevens, the lunch counter guy) surrounding him, greeting and fist-bumping him.

"What's *he* doing here?" I asked of no one.

No one answered.

I was going to go and see, but then he noticed me. He said something to the people around him and made his way over.

As he did, I noticed the girls at the next table, a bunch of seventh graders, whispering and giggling as they kept stealing glances at him. Rohan? They were checking him out like he was boyfriend material.

The guy I used to have flour fights with in the sweet shop who would then make me clean up? That was annoying-brother material.

"There you are, Sitara!" he said with a big smile as he got to my table. I could still hear the seventh graders whispering but tuned them out, especially when I heard one of them say, "... *mumble, mumble* ... so hot!"

Seriously? *Rohan?*

"Hi, Ro," Yael said. "What are you doing here?"

It didn't make sense that he was here at Knot's Valley Middle when he attended the high school down the road.

He motioned for me to sit down and took the empty spot across from Desmond, giving him a quick smile before he leaned across the table toward me.

"I'm on lunch too, but I wanted to come and tell you," he said, his eyes wide with excitement. "When I got back from the delivery this morning, you'll never guess who your mom was on the phone with."

I looked up at the ceiling. "Uhhhh, Wonder Woman?"

Rohan snorted. "Try again."

Pressing an index finger to the corner of my mouth, I said, "The lead singer from Chumz?"

He rolled his eyes. "Nope."

I huffed loudly. "Rohan, I have no idea, and lunch ends in, like, ten minutes. Why don't you just tell me?"

He leaned over the table even more, his eyes dancing. My friends leaned forward too. It felt as though the *whole cafeteria* was leaning toward Rohan, everyone holding their breath, waiting.

"Preeti Chandran," he finally said.

My mouth dropped open. I'd thought maybe the mayor or someone like that. Not someone *actually* super famous, like internationally, legit famous. Not someone I'd grown up watching. "Whoa, really?" I said, picturing the beautiful and SO glamorous actress in my head. My *mother* had talked to *the* Preeti Chandran?

"That's so cool," Yael said in a swoony voice. "What was she calling about?" While Yael wasn't Indian, she'd been my best friend forever, which meant she'd watched a bunch of Bollywood films and knew that Preeti Chandran was one of the top actresses. She'd been in most of my favorite childhood movies, and I'd already memorized the trailer for her next one: *Masala Madness.* She was what I call a VBD: a Very Big Deal.

Rohan went on, "Her fiancé's family is from here, and she's getting married in less than two weeks, but her baker had a family emergency and had to return to India. She made an appointment to come by the shop this afternoon to try everything out, and if she likes it, your parents will get to do all the baking and even her wedding cake!"

"Whoa," I said again but in a high-pitched squeak. This was seriously a VBD! Everyone knew she was coming to town for her upcoming wedding, but MY family's bakery might cater her wedding?! Then I realized the best part: I'd get to meet her! "My parents must be freaking out."

Rohan nodded vigorously, his eyebrows dancing. "They are. They're going to spend the day baking samples and getting ready. You're going to go help them after school, right?"

I glanced at Yael, who was staring at me. She widened her eyes.

"Uhhhhhh," I said. I don't know why I hesitated. This was Preeti Chandran!

Hiro's hazel eyes flashed in my mind. "I . . . I have drama club."

"Drama club?" Rohan said, leaning way back in his chair. "This is *Preeti Chandran*, Sitara. This is important. Your parents' business could explode if she uses them for her wedding and even just mentions it on social media. Do you know what this means?"

"Yes, of course I do," I said, fidgeting in my seat as he stared at me. "But I have drama club. I need to practice for the play. It's important." *And Hiro wants me there*, I didn't say. But that was a big part of it.

Rohan stood up, and I could tell from his frown that he was judging me. "I thought you'd be so excited. Especially since she's an actress and that's what you want to do. Not to mention you'd be helping your parents."

"Rohan," I said. "I *am* excited. *Of course* I want to meet her!"

He shook his head and then walked away, his shoulders slumped, clearly disappointed in me. And, well, he was right about Preeti Chandran, because she was a VBD. She wasn't a *Broadway* actress, like I wanted to be, but she was still very successful and SO famous! She'd been my idol before the summer I turned eight, when I discovered live theater like *Annie* and *Cats*. Meeting Preeti would be a dream come true.

But Hiro had specifically said I should be at drama club. With him.

Me and him. Together.

Eight-year-old Tara's dream versus thirteen-year-old Tara's dream.

My friends looked at me in sympathy.

"What are you going to do?" Gemma asked.

I looked down at my carrots and shrugged. "I have no idea. What *should* I do?"

*Tara goes home. Turn to page 23.*
23
*Tara goes to drama club. Turn to page 43.*
43

# Behind the Scenes

When I walked through the back door of the sweet shop after school that day, I felt like I was walking into a Kansas tornado. My mother was running around from the fryer to the prep table, then to the walk-in fridge and back again, muttering to herself. It seemed like every flat surface was covered in a million different treats: mini cakes, laddus, jalebi, cookies—nearly everything on our menu! She was a cyclone of icing sugar. All that was missing was the flying cow.

As I smiled at that thought, my attention was drawn to the back where Rohan was carrying in a bag of flour that was as big as me.

My dad was like the eye of the storm, standing at the long stainless-steel table in the middle of the kitchen, calmly icing brightly colored mandala cookies. Ugh. I wasn't psychic, but I knew what was coming if he was icing cookies. I slowly started to turn back to the door, already thinking about drama club, when—

"Sitara!" Mom barked. I lowered my backpack and turned to face her. She came over in a puff of nutmeg and gave me an awkward sort-of hug with her elbow before she flittered off to the fryer again. "Can you believe it: Preeti Chandran!" Without looking at me, she yelled in the same shrill voice, "I'm so glad you're here!"

"Me too. This is SO exciting!" I said. My parents had dreamed of running a successful sweet shop since even before I was born, and it did okay, but it wasn't like Starbucks successful yet, so I knew publicity thanks to a celebrity would help. A lot. It was thrilling to think their dreams would come true.

But I couldn't help but think of *my* dreams, and of Hiro, probably practicing lines right at that moment with Meg, my nemesis since last year, when they'd cast our class play of *Cinderella* and she got the title role. I'd been home sick with the flu, so *technically* she hadn't beat me out for the lead, but I had been stuck playing one of the mean stepsisters. Not exactly an opportunity to shine.

After school Hiro had passed me on the way to drama club. When I told him I couldn't make it, he'd given me his number so he could catch me up on what I'd missed. It was a great sign, but still, I would rather have been there with him.

At least Yael was still there and texting me updates. She'd already sent one to tell me that the drama teacher, Ms. Kinney, was going to add some extra drama club meetings for audition practice, which made me feel better about missing today's. *A little* better. I looked back up at the chaos, at my mom yelling at the stand mixer and my dad checking off a list as long as a Bollywood credit reel. Rohan had been right that this meeting was important to my parents. And of course, I would get to meet Preeti, which was still a VBD. Icing on the cake.

Mom waved a spatula toward Dad. "I need you to help your father with the cookies so he can finish the sample wedding cakes."

"How about I make some laddus instead," I

suggested hopefully. I hate icing cookies more than my most dreaded history class. *Especially* mandala cookies—they are so intricate and take so much concentration and steady hands. When I make laddus, I can sing and dance. When icing cookies, I have to do my best impression of a rusted Tin Man and keep very still. No thank you!

Dad looked up and shook his head while he stretched out his fingers. "The laddus are already done. We need the cookies finished now that the cakes are cool and ready to be decorated. Come on, Sitara; I've done most of the work—you just need to finish up the yellow, green, and orange icing."

He'd done most of the work. Right. I must have sighed out loud, because my mother said a very stern "Sitara!"

"Sorry," I mumbled as I made my way to the stairs so I could put my backpack away and grab a glass of juice before starting on the cookies.

"Where are you going!?" my mother shrieked. Seriously—she *shrieked* like a witch. And not like Glinda, the good witch.

I looked up for a wayward house whirling around overhead but then turned back toward her. "Uh, to put my books away and get something to drink—is that all right?"

She pointed at the chair in the corner. "Put your bag there. Get working. We don't have time, Sitara! Preeti Chandran is coming! PREETI CHANDRAN!"

She turned away, so she didn't see my eye roll (probably a good thing) as I dropped my bag and made my way over to the sink to slurp right from the tap. I wasn't actually thirsty; I had just hoped my dad would finish up with the cookies before I got back.

No such luck.

A while later my fingers were cramped, and my shoulders were stiff as I hunched over the counter. I was itching to be anywhere else other than drawing paisley designs on cookies with orange icing (without even music to hum to, because my parents thought listening to music distracted me).

My cell buzzed in my pocket. Happy for a break, I put the icing bag down on the counter and pulled out my phone, rolling out my shoulders to loosen them up.

As I'd hoped, it was a bunch of texts from

Yael. Des asked about you. Then she sent some heart and kiss emojis and: HE LIKES YOU.

I rolled my eyes. Yael *loved* matchmaking. But Paloma and Des made a good couple. I mean, he was pretty cute with his really blue eyes and freckly skin, and she'd said he was really smart, so she—GAK! My thoughts screeched to a halt as I saw Yael's next message.

TARA! H. FLIRTING w M.! He's calling her Dorothy and telling her she's going to get the part!

Oh no! What a disaster! It should have been *me* practicing with Hiro, not Meg. He should have been flirting with *me*!

I texted Yael back: DO SOMETHING!!!!

LIKE WHAT?

I typed out: Tell him I was born to be Dorothy. But then, as I waited for her to reply, I thought that maybe if I texted him myself, I could interrupt the flirting. Maybe I could distract him enough that he'd even flirt with *me* by text.

Never mind, I sent back to Yael. I'll text H.

Then I had a great idea. Want to rehearse on Friday after school? I sent Hiro.

I waited for him to answer but realized maybe he was busy flirting with Meg. Ugh!

I sent Yael another message. Tell H I'm texting

him and that it's important. Which was basically my way of getting him away from Meg.

A few minutes later he texted back: Great idea! You can come to my house after dinner!

*YESSSS!* I thought, doing a fist pump. Hiro Nakahara had just invited me—Sitara Singh—to his house!

As I began to tap out, C U then, Scarecrow, from your Dorothy, my heart was racing with crazy nerves. *You can do this,* I told myself. *Just be cool!*

But then Mom suddenly appeared beside me. "SITARA!" she barked, making me fumble my phone while I was still typing the message.

"Hold on," I said, but before I could finish my text, my mother swiped my phone RIGHT OUT OF MY HAND. "Hey!"

"Sitara, what did I tell you? This is important, and I need you to finish the cookies! You can text your friend later, after we have our meeting with Ms. Chandran."

"I'll only be a minute," I said, panic bubbling in my gut as I tried to get my phone. "It's important!"

Mom held the phone away from me and glared into my eyes. "I. Said. No. Finish the cookies like I asked, and then you can have your phone."

"But, Mom . . ."

She opened her mouth, and I knew she was getting mad, but I only needed my phone for a second. I'd come home after school to help, and all I wanted was one second!

"Sitara," Dad said sternly, coming up beside me. "You heard your mother. This meeting could change our lives." He took the phone from her and tucked it into his shirt pocket.

"Cookies aren't the only thing that's important, you know!" I blurted out in frustration. "I just need one second to send a text, and then I'll do the stupid cookies. I'm here helping out when I should have been in drama club, and now I'm not going to get to be Dorothy and . . . Meg and . . . Ugh . . . everything is *ruined!*" And then, just because, I smashed my fist down on one of the cookies, crushing it into a colorful, crumbly mess.

My parents just stood there, blinking at me while I breathed hard. I was in for it now.

Suddenly someone cleared their throat at the front of the store.

OMG. Preeti Chandran did *not* just hear me yell at my parents. But as I held my breath and chanced a glance over, I was relieved to see it was only Rohan.

Until I saw the horrified look on his face. He'd clearly heard my freak-out and was not impressed. I suddenly felt like Yael's sister, who was two and a half and had ginormous tantrums when she didn't get her way.

I realized that maybe there was a teeny tiny, munchkin-size chance that I had overreacted.

Rohan cleared his throat again and said, "Ms. Chandran just called to say she's on her way over." Then he turned and went back to the front of the store, pulling the door mostly closed behind him.

I looked down at the scattered crumbs on the floor and waited for the inevitable.

My mother took a deep breath as I held mine, expecting to be grounded. Or worse. "Sitara," she said. "Look at me."

Her voice was calm. I lifted my head.

"We do appreciate that you missed out on drama club to be here to help us."

I slowly exhaled, knowing there was more coming.

"However," she said, giving me one of her very serious looks. *Here we go.* "That is no reason for you to disrespect us by speaking the way you did. What do you say for yourself?"

"Sorry," I muttered, biting my tongue on the

rest of what I wanted to say, which was *Can I have my phone back now?* because I knew asking would do the opposite of getting me my phone back.

"And?" Dad said.

*And what?* "And I'll finish the cookies," I said.

"And," Dad said again, pointing at the crumbs on the floor.

"And," I said, fighting the sigh that wanted so badly to come out, "I will clean up the mess."

Mom gave me a satisfied nod. "Good. Now I'm going upstairs to change; I'll be back in a few minutes."

Dad returned to the sample cakes, arranging them on a big platter. Amazed that I hadn't gotten in more trouble (but not about to question it), I reached for the icing bag, gritting my teeth when my phone buzzed in Dad's pocket. I may as well have set the ringtone to "torture."

He pulled the phone out, and I was suddenly elated, sure he was going to hand it to me, but instead, and to my GREATEST HORROR, he looked at the screen. No, not just *looked* at the screen but was staring at it, reading!

"Dad!" I screeched. "That's private!"

I reached to snatch it out of his hand, but he

just held it up over my head while he continued reading.

"Dad!" I yelled again, because he was reading my private information that was probably about Hiro.

"When you earn respect, you will get it," Dad said, one of his favorite sayings. "Also, last time I checked, I pay for this phone."

I couldn't argue unless I wanted to take all the money I made at the sweet shop and spend it on phone bills, which I didn't. But still, he was totally invading my privacy!

*Please give me back my phone, please give me back my phone,* I chanted in my head. *Please. Give. Me. Back. My. Phone!*

"Huh," Dad said as he finally stopped reading and frowned at me. "What does this scarecrow and dog stuff mean? That doesn't make sense."

"Wha—?" I asked, because he was right that it made no sense.

He held my phone up in front of me and pointed at the screen where the text window was still open. The last message was from Hiro: The only thing in it was a dog emoji and the word "woof." Huh?

What was he talking about? But wait. I looked

at the message above his. *Oh no . . .* It appeared I had texted him: From your Dog.

NOOOOOOO!

I covered my face with my hands just as the bell on the front door of the shop jingled.

I heard Rohan's excited voice as he greeted the super-famous VBD star.

Seriously? Could I not catch a break?

"It's showtime," Dad said with a big smile, sliding my phone back into his pocket right before he grabbed my hand and led me out to the front of the shop.

"It smells so good in here!" Preeti was saying in her beautiful voice. "If your sweets taste half as good as they smell, I am going to—" She broke off as she turned and noticed me in the doorway. "Oh, hello. And who is this?"

She was absolutely stunning—even more beautiful in real life than on the screen, if that was possible. She was wearing a traditional Indian outfit, a *shalwar kameez*—a long, purple-patterned top and teal pants underneath, with a matching gauzy scarf that flowed behind her. Her red-black hair was long and shiny, and her eye makeup was smoky and dramatic, making her brown eyes pop.

She seemed larger than life, even though she was as petite as my mom.

My mouth was suddenly so dry, it was like it was full of flour. I swallowed and took a deep breath, trying to sort out what to say to her, except everything sounded so stupid in my head.

"Don't be shy," she said, gesturing me forward with her hand.

I have *never* been shy, but at that moment, standing right in front of the most beautiful and talented Bollywood actress in the world, I was suddenly . . . utterly . . . shy. My dad gave me a little shove with his hand on my back, and said, "I'm Gani Singh. This is my daughter, Sitara, and you've met Rohan."

Preeti nodded and glanced over at Rohan, who was looking as starstruck as I felt, standing nervously behind the glass case.

The tall man beside Preeti (who I hadn't noticed until just that second) looked between Rohan and me and said, "You're brother and sister?"

Rohan's eyes widened into dinner plates. "No!" he blurted. "I mean, we're not related. I just work here."

Preeti's lips curved into a smile as she turned

back to me. "It's lovely to meet you, Sitara," she said before smiling at my dad and extending an elegant hand toward him. "And you as well, Gani."

Dad took her hand and shook it vigorously in both of his. "It's such a pleasure to meet you, Ms. Chandran. We're all such huge fans! Sitara wants to be an actress someday, and you've been such an inspiration to her."

*DAD!* I wanted to yell, except all I could do was try to smile at Preeti while feeling my face get as hot as if there were a million stage lights on me.

She dipped her head, her smile getting wider. "Thank you so much. It's an honor to know I've inspired other actors. Maybe someday we can chat about it."

Whaaaaaaat? Did she just say she wanted to talk to *me*? About *acting*???

I just stood there, stunned, while she went on, "And please, you must call me Preeti." She took the arm of the man beside her. "And this is my fiancé, Sanjit Pradesh."

"I'm just here for the cake," he announced, making everyone laugh.

Suddenly there was a commotion behind us, a *thump-thump-thump* down the back stairs from our apartment. Two seconds later Mom came busting in, out of breath, wearing one of her best saris and a fresh coat of lipstick. "Oh! I'm so sorry to keep you waiting! I'm Reha; we spoke on the phone."

"No trouble at all," Preeti said. "Lovely to meet you in person. Now, I was promised plenty of goodies, and Sanjit is clearly eager for some, so should we get started?"

Mom nodded, still catching her breath, and then led Preeti and Sanjit into the bakery, where everything was set up. I hung back, still feeling like a silly fangirl, not sure what to say to her. I mean, she was so nice, but I didn't want to blurt out anything stupid. She was SO famous!

Rohan must have felt the same, because he stayed with me at the front of the store, watching through the doorway as Preeti glided to the table where she began to ooh and aah over everything. Dad then started talking about the different cakes while Preeti seemed to hang on his every word. She was nodding along like he was saying the most interesting things in the world.

"I'm glad you came to help out," Rohan said quietly.

*I'm not,* I almost said, thinking about Hiro. And Meg. And the dumb text I'd sent by accident.

But then I realized I'd just met a famous actress, and Meg hadn't. "Me too, I guess," I said.

"Sitara?" Dad interrupted, getting our attention. "Ms. Chandran—Preeti—is asking about the mandala cookies. Can you come show her how you ice them?"

I glanced over at Rohan, who waggled his eyebrows at me. Weirdo.

Preeti and Sanjit tasted everything, and it was obvious by their oohs and aahs and all their yummy noises that their delight was not an act. To our excitement, they placed a huge order for the wedding.

After they had left, and we had jumped up and down (me and Mom) and thumped the tables (Rohan and Dad) and whooped and hollered (all of us), Mom and Dad went upstairs to get some rest before they had to start baking for the next day. Rohan and I told them we'd clean up. They were very grateful, but not grateful enough to give back my phone. It was still tucked into Dad's shirt, and there was nothing I could do to get it back before we finished cleaning and I joined them upstairs.

I was wiping down the last of the counters when Rohan started mopping the floor on the other side of the kitchen. "She's cool, huh?" he said as he worked.

I nodded, walking the cloth over to the sink to shake out the crumbs. "I didn't think she'd be so nice."

"Right?" Rohan agreed. "It's crazy that they thought we were related, huh?"

I turned to look at him. "What?"

"You know, that they thought we were brother and sister. I mean, I sure don't think of you as a *sister*. Ha-ha!" His face was a little pink when he said it, but maybe it was from the mopping—he did seem to be working very hard at it.

"Rohan?"

He stopped and straightened up, resting his hands on the end of the mop handle. "Huh?"

"What's going on?" I asked. "You're being so strange today."

His face got even redder. He looked away for a long, awkward moment and then returned his gaze to me. He reached into his back pocket and pulled out a ticket. "Well, I was going to save this for later, but I got tickets to see *Masala Madness* this Friday night—it's debuting in North America—and I thought . . . well, I thought, um, maybe we could go together?"

Wait. He was asking me to go see Preeti's newest movie with him? Was he asking me on *a date*? Was that why he was being so weird? SO MANY questions went through my head in that second, but they were all versions of the same thing:

Did *Rohan* like me?

Did Rohan *like* me, as in girlfriend-and-boyfriend like me?

Did Rohan really like *me*, Tara Singh, middle schooler and family friend?

Before I could take any of those thoughts further, I realized there was a problem. I was supposed to practice for the audition with Hiro on Friday. "Uh, I can't; I have to rehearse on Friday, and it's important." *Mostly because of Hiro*, I didn't say, but also: "I already missed today's drama club, so I need to catch up."

He gave me a sly smile. "Even if Preeti is coming to the screening and will be doing a talk after, like they do at film festivals?"

"Oh, that's . . . ," I drawled. That sounded pretty cool. But what about my plans with Hiro?

"*Aaaaand* even if she said she was looking forward to seeing us there?"

"Shut up!" I yelled, smacking his arm. "She did not say that."

Rohan nodded. "She did. When she came up front to pay the deposit."

I put my hand on my hip and cocked my head as I glared at him. "Are you lying to me, Rohan?"

He looked into my eyes and held up his palm toward me as he shook his head. "I promise I'm not. I told her I'd bought the tickets, and that's when she said it was a big surprise that she'd be there. No one but the theater owner—and I guess me and now you—knows, but she said she looked forward to seeing us. I wanted to surprise you, but I don't want you to miss out by going to your drama thing. . . ." He shrugged.

My "drama thing" was a big deal. Maybe even a date. But . . . Preeti was a VBD. And maybe she'd help me with my acting; she'd already said we could chat about it. Would she be upset if I didn't go, or would she understand how important rehearsing was and respect my commitment?

And what would Hiro think if I bailed a second time? I pretty much knew what he'd think: He'd think I didn't want to be the Dorothy to his Scarecrow. Which wasn't true, because I *did* want to be Dorothy. Bad. *Really* bad. And maybe even worse than that, maybe he'd think I didn't like him.

What was I supposed to do?

Rehearse with Hiro or go to the movie with Rohan?

---

*Tara goes to Hiro's house. Turn to page 103.*
*Tara goes to the movies. Turn to page 58.*

# In the Wings

"Do you think Rohan was really mad at you?" Yael asked as we walked together toward the school auditorium after last-period gym. We'd hurried to get changed after basketball, so we'd actually beaten the bell by a few minutes. Yael had a while before her mom came to pick her up to take her to Hebrew school, so she was keeping me company on the walk to the theater. "He seemed pretty upset about you bailing on your parents to go to drama club."

I winced. "I'm not bailing." But that was a lie. Even though my parents hadn't said I *had* to go home to help them, I knew they would have appreciated it. They had to be freaking out if someone like Preeti Chandran was coming to do a tasting and was thinking of using them to cater her wedding. So yeah, I felt like I was bailing, especially when Rohan had gone on and on about it, making me feel worse.

And then there was *Preeti Chandran*. It would have been really cool to meet her, a legit actress, but kind of scary at the same time, because she was SO FAMOUS. What would I have said to her? Would she have thought I was some sort of wannabe? And anyway, wouldn't *she* do whatever it takes to get a role? Of course she would.

Coming to drama club meant I was following my dream, and everyone always says you should follow your dreams no matter what, right? Especially if those dreams mean you get to act with a cute boy. Boys can be parts of dreams; I was pretty sure of it. That's why they say cute boys are *dreamy*.

"Well, I hope he's not *too* mad," Yael said. "But he needs to understand that the sweet shop isn't the only thing going on in your life. He's so . . ." She scrunched up her face and shrugged.

"Responsible?" I offered.

"No." She frowned. "Boring, more like."

I didn't think Rohan was boring, but I got what she was saying. He could *seem* boring, but he was just really into practical things. Which, as I thought about it more, maybe *was* boring.

Once we got to the auditorium, Yael wished me luck, and by the wag of her eyebrows I knew she was wishing me luck more with Hiro than with the rehearsing. I gave her a quick hug before going into the theater.

There was a table by the door with a pile of photocopied pages of TWOz scripts on it, so I grabbed one and made my way down the aisle toward the stage. I was the first one there, so I took a seat in the middle to study the lines while I waited for everyone.

I'd only just gotten into the script when the seat next to me squeaked as someone slid onto it. I turned to smile at Hiro, except it wasn't him after all. It was Desmond.

I looked around the theater at the million empty seats—why was he sitting right next to me?

"Uh . . . hi," he said.

"Hi," I said back, looking past him to see Hiro and a bunch of other kids come in and sit down by the stage on the other side of the center aisle.

Great, and I was blocked in by Desmond.

Then, while I was trying to figure out how to get past Desmond without being totally rude, Meg Hamilton strode in and sat *right next to Hiro*! Ugh!

"All right, everyone, take a seat," Ms. Kinney, our drama teacher, called out as she came in and walked down the aisle toward the stage. Once she got to the front, she turned around and faced us. "I presume everyone heard about the Knot's Valley Little Theater's upcoming production of *The Wizard of Oz*?"

Excited murmurs went up from the crowd.

"Right, and who is auditioning?"

I thrust up my hand and looked around. Nearly everyone else had their hand up too. Not Desmond, though. Actually, I wasn't sure what he was doing there. He wasn't even *in* drama club. Shouldn't he be up in the lighting booth or something?

"Okay," Ms. Kinney said, sweeping her eyes around the room. "Since that's pretty much all of you, we may as well spend some time practicing for auditions. I printed out a short part of the script; if anyone didn't get one, they're on the table by the door."

A bunch of people scrambled to the back of the theater to grab scripts. Of course, I already had mine.

"So," Ms. Kinney went on when everyone was seated again. "Does anyone have experience with doing auditions—community theater or even commercials or modeling?"

No one raised their hand, which made me feel better about my lack of real-life auditioning experience. But I shook off my doubt—I was born to be Dorothy! I had watched TWOz approximately seven hundred times. I'd even dressed up as her for Halloween two times in a row, complete with braids and gingham dress.

"All right," Ms. Kinney said. "So we'll start with the basics. They will probably have you sing something if you're trying out for a singing part, but even if not, they'll have you run lines, likely with partners. Everyone pair up and take ten minutes to go over the scene, then we can get started onstage."

I stood quickly to team up with Hiro, but before I could even make a move to push past Desmond, Meg was clutching Hiro's arm possessively.

Opportunity missed. Grrr. Desmond!

I looked around, but while I'd been stuck in

my row, everyone had quickly found someone—I was the odd person out. Unless you counted Desmond.

I looked at him, and he cleared his throat.

Perfect. Now I was going to have to go up and read lines with the super-shy guy who made the Cowardly Lion look like the bravest guy in the world! How was I supposed to shine with a total fraidycat for a partner?

"So I guess you're going to read with me?" I said, sounding a little whiny, but seriously, he'd ruined everything! It was supposed to be *me* over there with Hiro, not my nemesis, rotten Meg Hamilton.

Desmond's eyes went wide. "Oh, uh, no. I don't act; I just wanted to say hi. But I'm sure you'll do great—you always shine."

And then, before I could say anything else (not that I had anything to say other than *Thanks a lot for NOTHING!*), he scurried away toward the door to the control booth at the back of the theater and disappeared through it.

I took my script over to where Hiro and Meg were practicing.

"Hey, Tara," Hiro said, smiling up at me.

"Can I practice with you?" I asked.

Hiro opened his mouth, but Meg butted in. "No, we're already paired up. Find someone else."

Ugh. Did she have to be so mean? "There's an odd number. The three of us can work together."

"Yeah, I don't think so," Meg said, and then narrowed her eyes at me.

I glared right back at her, but she leaned closer to Hiro, gave me a smug look, and said, "Go practice with the teacher."

I looked at Hiro, and he just shrugged like there was nothing he could do.

I sighed and turned away from them and was going to ask the teacher to read with me, but she was striding with authority over to two kids who were jumping off the backs of some theater seats and shrieking out some surprisingly good— and loud—witch cackles. Maybe reading with Desmond would have been better than being stuck alone. I sat down by myself and went over the lines a few times in my head before pulling my phone out to look at it, hoping that someone had texted me.

Thankfully, someone had. It wasn't Yael, though, but Rohan to tell me that Preeti was so nice and had loved my samosas.

That's great! I texted back to him.

She's going to use the sweet shop for her wedding! Rohan sent.

My jaw dropped. I wanted to squeal but saw the cacklers getting reprimanded. My parents' little sweet shop was going to be FAMOUS! I texted Rohan a string of exclamation points.

And the best part . . .

I waited for him to type, but it seemed to take FOREVER!

Rohan! The anticipation is killing me!

She's going to be at the local premiere of Masala Madness on Friday taking questions like at a film festival! Want to go?

Did I want to go? Was he kidding? *Of course* I wanted to go! Like he had to even ask!?

But wait. He *had* asked.

Movies were date things. Did that mean he wanted it to be a date? Was he asking me just as a friend or because he liked me and wanted us to go as boyfriend and girlfriend? I glanced over at Hiro, who was laughing with Meg. It didn't look like they were even reading the script.

I looked back at my phone. If I said yes to Rohan and it was a date, what did that mean about my chances with Hiro?

I wanted to see Preeti so badly, especially since

I'd missed meeting her today. And what would be cooler than having her in person at the premiere, talking about her movie and answering questions?

Ugh. I needed to think about it. Actually, I needed to think and talk to Yael about it. *She* would know what to do.

Must go—time to read my lines! I sent back to Rohan before slipping the phone into my bag, not waiting for an answer from him that might just confuse things more.

A few moments later the readings began.

The first ones ranged from totally, cringe-worthily awful to okay and even good. Not good enough to make me *really* worried, but enough to make me realize I needed to practice because I might not be a shoo-in.

Finally, it was time for Hiro and Meg. I held my breath as they got up there and took their spots, grinning at each other in a way that made me want to barf because, please.

They got about seven lines in when the strangest thing happened. Meg broke character and turned toward the audience, pressing her palms against her eyes. Her lip quivered, and it looked like she was going to cry, and I suddenly felt bad for her.

"Ms. Kinney! I . . . UGH! Can I start again?" she wailed.

"Just keep going," Ms. Kinney said. "You were almost done. Hiro, lead her in with your last line."

But it was obvious that Meg had lost her momentum. Even though Hiro backtracked and read the line before hers, she stuttered and stumbled on the lines. She could barely finish the scene before she ran offstage and all the way out of the theater while Hiro stood there, dumbstruck. If that was what her real audition was going to be like, I seriously had nothing to worry about.

"What happened?" Hiro asked, scratching his head.

"Welcome to live theater," Ms. Kinney said. "Things happen. You need to be able to roll with them. Katy, can you please go make sure Meg's okay? Bring her back, if you can."

Katy nodded and left the auditorium while Ms. Kinney looked around. "Okay, who do we have left?"

The last to go, I lifted my hand. "Just me."

"Hiro, you didn't really get to practice. Why don't you read with Tara?"

Yes! Now was my chance to show him I was WAY better than Meg.

I walked up the few stairs and stepped onto the stage. Suddenly all the overhead lights went off.

There was a collective gasp from the audience. Then, all of a sudden, with a click and a hum, a spotlight blazed on. And it was focused right on me.

When I got my bearings, I walked over toward Hiro, and like a shadow (or, I guess, the *opposite* of a shadow), the spotlight followed me to the center of the stage. I had to suppress a smile, because I had a sudden feeling who was behind it. The guy who'd told me I always shine was making it happen for real.

And I kind of loved it. No, I *really* loved it. I really loved it *a lot*.

"All right, all right," Ms. Kinney said, and got up on the stage. She shielded her eyes with her hand and looked up toward the control booth. "Can we have the overhead lights back on, please?"

A moment later my spotlight was gone, but my confidence wasn't. I turned to Hiro and started our scene, channeling my Dorothy as he became the Scarecrow.

It was just a short section of their first meeting, so it was over before I got really into it, but

I knew I'd given my best performance ever, not just because *I* felt it, but because the entire drama club broke into thunderous applause.

Hiro and I faced the crowd. He took a bow, and I did a polite curtsy.

"Well done, you two," Ms. Kinney said. "All right, come on down. We can take a ten-minute break, and then we'll do another round. We're going to change things up so you really stretch your acting skills."

Hiro bounded down off the stage, but as I moved to follow him, I took a second to smile up at the control booth, silently thanking Desmond for my spotlight.

Once we got back from break, Ms. Kinney made us switch partners and roles, telling us that being great actors meant preparing for parts outside our comfort zones.

I was determined to roll with things, as Ms. Kinney had advised, so when I got assigned to be Toto to Denny Lyle's Dorothy, I played it up and didn't just act like Toto—I *became* Toto. And when Toto met the Tin Man (Hiro), I even pretended to pee on his leg. Everyone in the audience howled with laughter (except the Tin Man, who didn't break character but made an attempt to sidestep and then stiffened up as though he were rusting).

Even Ms. Kinney applauded, shaking her head as she smiled up at us. "Nicely done," she said. "You really committed there."

Hiro smiled at me and gave me a *woof*, which I took to mean he'd liked my performance too. By the time we came down off the stage and let the next group go up, Meg had returned from the bathroom with red-rimmed eyes. She refused to read again, which meant *she* was the odd one out this time.

In the end, Ms. Kinney told us we were all contenders for parts (which I think was a tiny white lie but was nice of her to say) and reminded us to keep practicing at home in between drama club meetings because we could never be too prepared for auditions.

We were all getting ready to leave when Hiro came up to me.

"Hey," I said, pretending it was no big deal, even though I was quivering on the inside in anticipation of him talking to me.

"Hey, Toto, want to come over to my place on Friday night?"

I laughed at him calling me Toto, even though I really would have rather he call me Dorothy. But had he just asked me to come over? To his house?

"So, how about it?" he said, giving me a really cute smile, a lock of his black hair flopping over his forehead. "You know, to practice for the audition."

"Oh, yeah, of course," I said, hoping my face wasn't as red as it felt. Not possible, because it felt like lava was running through my veins.

Except something was sticking in my brain. Friday night. Friday night . . .

Wait! Friday was the premiere of *Masala Madness*! The one Rohan had invited me to. The one Preeti herself would be at that I *really* wanted to go to.

"Uh, I'd like to, but I have a thing. How about Thursday?"

Hiro frowned. "Nope, sorry. I have lacrosse Thursday."

"Saturday?" I said, hopeful. *Reeeeeeeeally* hopeful.

But Hiro shook his head. "I'm at my dad's from Saturday morning until Sunday night. So, Friday?"

Sigh. Friday.

What on earth was I supposed to do?

———————————

*Tara goes to Hiro's house. Turn to page 103.*
*Tara goes to the movies. Turn to page 72.*

# Breaking Character

"Do you want to get some popcorn?" Rohan asked on Friday evening once we got inside the movie theater.

Like he needed to ask? "Is a movie without popcorn really a movie?"

He laughed. "Okay, okay."

As we made our way through the theater, I noticed one of the big *Masala Madness* posters with Preeti's smiling face on it. I did a little Bollywood hip sway and twirl on the way to the snack counter, waggling my eyebrows at Rohan.

He laughed, and we got in line behind two

other couples. Which made me wonder, for about the eight millionth time, if *we* were a couple. As in, did he think this was a date? I looked at him out of the corner of my eye; he was busy getting his wallet out of his jacket pocket. That was a good sign. A *very* good sign.

"If he pays for everything," Yael had told me earlier at school, "it's a date. If he just asked you as a friend, he'll make you pay for your own stuff." It seemed like a good way to figure it out, and Yael watches a lot of romantic movies, so she knew what she was talking about.

So far Rohan had paid for the tickets, but as Yael had pointed out, he'd already had them when he'd invited me, so maybe he'd bought them expecting one of his friends to go with him, but they had canceled. That meant I couldn't use the tickets as evidence that this was a date. But how we paid for the popcorn would solve everything.

The couple ahead of us got their snacks, and then it was our turn. We stepped up to the counter, and he turned toward me. "Popcorn and a root beer?"

Did it mean anything that he knew root beer was my favorite? "Yes, please." I nodded and reached for my purse, because Yael had wisely suggested I should make it *look* like I expected to pay for myself. That way, when he said, *I'll pay*, I would know for sure it was a date and not just him paying because it seemed like I expected him to.

"One large popcorn and two root beers, please," he said to the guy at the counter.

*One* popcorn! That meant we would be sharing. That *had* to mean it was a date, right?

Rohan turned to me. "I only want a little, so it makes sense to share, if you don't mind."

"Oh, yeah, right, makes total sense. I don't mind at all," I said, and then held my breath as I fumbled around in my purse for my wallet, purposely not finding it right away to give him a chance to—

"I've got this, Sitara," he said. "You can put your wallet away."

Whoa. He paid! It's a date!

As he handed the guy his money, I took the giant bucket of popcorn and my drink. I was happy for something to do with my hands because SWEET SAMOSAS, THIS WAS A DATE! Now that it was really real, a million thoughts went around in my head, like: *Does this mean he's my*

*boyfriend? What about Hiro? And most impor-*
*tantly, will Rohan, the guy I've known forever, try*
*to kiss me? Do I want him to? Will it be weird?*

We walked side by side, and I felt like I should
say something. Anything. But I was suddenly
nervous and unsure what to talk about, afraid if I
opened my mouth, stupid things might come out.
My being quiet was new, because usually I talked
nonstop around him.

But there was one thing that was safe to say:
"Thanks for paying for the snacks."

"No problem," he said, smiling at me. "Actually,
I didn't really pay. When I told your mom that we
were coming tonight, she insisted on paying and
gave me some money. So really, you should thank
her when you get home."

*MOM!* My heart plummeted into my belly at
that. How was I *ever* supposed to know if this
was a date? Though I bet my mother thought/
hoped it was.

As we walked into the theater and looked up at
the seats, I saw a bunch of girls from school—the
whispering seventh graders from the cafeteria—
sitting in a row in the middle. As they saw us, they
huddled together, and I could imagine exactly
what they were thinking: *There's Tara Singh with*

*that cute high school guy. They must be on a date!*

They might be right; if only *I* knew for sure.

"That was amazing!" I said as the credits began and the lights came on.

Rohan was grinning, and his eyes were wide—just as entranced by the movie as I was. "Right? So good."

The crowd in the theater started getting ready to leave when a man came out to the front of the seats with a microphone in his hand.

"Everyone, may I have your attention, please?"

As people settled down, waiting for him to make his announcement, Rohan and I looked at each other knowingly. He even winked at me, which made me have to look away from him, focusing my eyes on the man with the microphone, because Rohan had never winked at me before! What did a wink mean?! Was it a date signal?

I had no time to think about it as the theater guy spoke: "We have a special treat for you all. We have none other than the star of *Masala Madness*, Preeti Chandran, here to say a few words about the film!"

An excited murmur went through the

crowd, which suddenly turned into a standing ovation as Preeti came out from a side door. She looked amazing, as always, her diamond nose ring glittering in the overhead light, her makeup dramatic and perfect. Rohan and I grinned at each other. We knew her! She was wearing a saffron-yellow outfit, and she strutted with confidence up to the man. She nodded at him as she took the microphone and then smiled up at the packed audience.

"Thank you so much! I'm so honored. Please, please, have a seat." She gestured for everyone to sit and waited before she went on. "As some of you may know, my fiancé is from this area, so after my wedding, I will be spending a lot of time—when I'm not on set—here in Knot's Valley. Already I feel so welcome here and look forward to becoming a true member of the community."

A roar went up from the crowd; then someone stuck up their hand.

Preeti smiled at the girl. "Yes?"

"I heard a rumor that you were going to be starting up an acting program for youth at the community center—is that true?"

"Wow, word really travels in small towns, doesn't it?" Preeti said with a chuckle. "There is some truth to that, but it's still in the works. That's all I can say for now."

I looked at Rohan with giant eyes. He mouthed, "Whoa." I couldn't have written this script better! I wasn't the only one who was thrilled—there was loud cheering and a chorus of "Yesssss!" in the theater.

Preeti continued. "I just have to get through my wedding first. Acting like a cool and calm bride is probably my most difficult role to date," she said, making everyone laugh.

She went on to talk about the film and even answered a bunch of questions from the crowd, making me love her as a person and not just an actress. She was so nice and such a pro—a real inspiration. I said as much to Rohan as we were leaving the theater.

He looked over at me. "So you're still on that acting kick, huh?"

"Not just acting," I said. "Singing and dancing, too."

He smiled. "Well, you do have an amazing voice."

There was that compliment again, the one that made me wonder how long I hadn't noticed him noticing me. "Thanks," I said.

He looked around and then leaned in close, really close, making my heart thump like a *dhol* drum. "Maybe even more amazing than Preeti's."

I instantly froze, making the girl walking behind me smash into my back.

"Watch out!" she said, and then darted her eyes at Rohan before she mumbled something and took off.

I recognized her as one of the swoony seventh graders and snorted before returning to what Rohan had just said. "You don't mean that. I don't have a better voice than Preeti."

"I do mean it," he assured me as he nodded toward the exit to get me moving again. "You'll be a Bollywood star, I have no doubt in my mind."

I laughed loudly. "Bollywood? No way," I said. "I'm going to be on Broadway! Step one: Nail the audition for *The Wizard of Oz* next Saturday."

He did a double take.

"What?" I asked, because he looked almost . . . hurt.

Grabbing my arm, he led me out of the crowd, moving toward the door and over to the wall. "What do you have against Bollywood?"

When had I said anything against Bollywood? We'd just watched a Bollywood movie! "Nothing, but I want to be on Broadway and do shows like *Hamilton*. Or maybe *Wicked*, which would be perfect since I'm already an expert on TWOz."

"Twoz?"

I rolled my eyes. "*The Wizard of Oz*, obviously."

"Sitara . . ." He shook his head. "Broadway is cool, but . . ."

I crossed my arms. "But what?"

"Bollywood is . . . well, it's you. It's us."

I rolled my eyes. "Please, Rohan. You sound old, like my parents."

He frowned at that. "It's not an old thing. It's about traditions. Our culture is important to me. It should be to you, too. Why would you want to turn your back on our heritage?"

"I'm not turning my back on anything," I said, starting to walk again. I suddenly didn't like this conversation. How had it gone from him saying that I was a better singer than Preeti Chandran to telling me I needed to give up my dreams of Broadway and be a Bollywood actress. He was acting like that was my *job* because my family was from India. He didn't understand at all!

We got to the lobby, and I told him I needed to use the bathroom, mostly because things had gotten so confusing and weird, and all the good feelings about being there with him and seeing Preeti were gone.

I didn't wait for him to say anything before I ducked into the bathroom. I pulled out my phone to text Yael but then realized it was Friday night. Since she's Jewish, her parents make her power down her phone on Shabbat. It didn't matter. I didn't need her to know that this was definitely not a date. It was a Bollywood intervention.

Dramatic sigh.

I opened up the text window with Hiro, but he hadn't sent anything. At least not since I'd told him I wasn't coming to his place to rehearse after all. (He'd responded to that with a "woof." Even after I'd explained to him in class about my texting fail and what I'd meant to say, he wouldn't let it go and had started calling me Toto and randomly barked at me. It was cool to share an inside joke. I guess.)

I tucked the phone back into my purse and stood in front of the mirror, trying to figure out how to fix things with Rohan, or at least make them less weird. I heard the buzz of a new text.

I pulled out my cell again. Hiro? Nope. Desmond.

Hey Tara, Hiro told me you were going to come

over to rehearse with him, but then said you canceled. You still going to try out for Dorothy? You're SO much better than Meg!

So random. But so, so nice. Paloma had gushed about how sweet he was. Then I realized he was saying Hiro had talked about me. I wondered if he was disappointed I'd canceled!

Thank you! Yes, I'm still trying out, I sent him.

Awesome! U will crush it! he texted back immediately.

I hoped he was right. I suddenly had a terrible image of me at the audition, watching everyone cheer for Meg as she won the starring role. I put my phone away and quickly went back out into the lobby before Rohan thought I was sick or something.

He was waiting for me against the far wall, a guilty look on his face. He pushed away and came toward me. "Hey. I'm sorry that I made you feel bad about your dreams, Sitara," he said, then looked down at his feet as we made our way to the doors. "I just . . . I guess I'm just traditional and forget not everyone thinks like me."

"It's okay," I said. "I'll still send you tickets when I'm on Broadway."

He laughed.

I looked up at him and noticed he wasn't as

scrawny as I remembered. Did Rohan . . . lift weights? I focused on a movie poster just above his shoulder. His surprisingly muscular shoulder. "But until then . . . um . . . maybe you could come see me when I'm Dorothy in the Knot's Valley production."

He glanced over at me, the frown back on his face.

"About that," he said. "Did you say auditions were next Saturday, like, a week from tomorrow?"

"Yeah. So?"

"That's the same day as Preeti's wedding. You were planning to help out your parents, weren't you?"

I knew they wanted me there, but they also told me to do what I thought best. And not in a guilt-trippy way. They were good like that. And I *really* wanted to go to the audition. But as I looked at Rohan, I could tell that was not the answer he was expecting. When I didn't say anything, he shook his head.

"Sitara, your parents are depending on you. Not to mention that it's Preeti."

I shrugged. "Just because she's a celebrity . . ." A Bollywood *celebrity*, I didn't say, but the truth was that while Bollywood actors were a big deal to us, they weren't a big deal to the whole world, especially the Broadway world.

"But just think of the opportunities. Just because you don't want to go into Bollywood doesn't mean she wouldn't know people in other areas of acting. She could really help you."

Ugh, I hated it when Rohan made good points!

I had a good point of my own, though. "But the audition . . . that would help me more if I got an *actual* acting role."

He made a *ffft* noise. "It's just a little community theater—it doesn't really count. And there will be other roles. But Preeti . . . you heard what she said about her acting program. Also, you know her fiancé is a producer, too, right?"

I did *not* know that. "Really?"

He held the door open for me and nodded at me to go through ahead of him. "Yes, really— that's how they met after he left here and went to work in India. I mean, I get that you want to be in the play, but I think you should go to the wedding."

"Rohan . . ."

"I *really* think you should go, Sitara." He dropped his eyes and added, "For lots of reasons."

What he was saying made sense, I guess. He

was so practical all the time, but sometimes it was like he thought only with his head. Didn't he ever make decisions with his heart?

Although, right now my own heart was so torn.

What was I going to do?

---

*Tara goes to the audition. Turn to page 116.*
*Tara goes to the wedding. Turn to page 88.*

# Rom-Com DRAMA

"Sitara?"

I looked over at Rohan, realizing he must have said something and was waiting for an answer.

Oops.

We'd just walked into the movie theater, which was decked out in colorful *Masala Madness* posters of a smiling Preeti wearing a purple-and-gold sari in the arms of her handsome costar. I had been distracted, both by the posters and then by wondering if Hiro would have liked to have come. Did I miss an opportunity by not inviting him?

Except, that's where things got complicated:

If Rohan thought this was a date, he wouldn't have liked it if *I* had brought a date. But if I hadn't been here with Rohan to see Preeti and her movie, I'd be at Hiro's house, rehearsing for the TWOz audition. That would have been cool. Really cool. Like, date-with-my-ultimate-crush-who-is-cute-and-loves-to-act type cool.

Instead, here I was with Rohan, who's a nice guy and all, but . . .

Oops again. He was still staring at me, waiting for my answer to, um, something.

"Sorry, Rohan," I said, shaking off thoughts of Hiro and dating. At least for the moment. "I was distracted by the movie posters; I still can't believe Preeti is using our shop to cater her wedding. What did you say?"

"I know, right?" he said, smiling. "I asked if you want popcorn. We can share some."

"Oh, right. Sure," I said. "Thanks."

"Something wrong?" he asked as we made our way through the busy lobby filled with other people excited to see the local premiere of *Masala Madness*.

"Oh." I looked over at him and put on a smile. "No. Just thinking about the audition next week, that's all." I wasn't about to tell him I'd been thinking about *the boy* I would be auditioning with.

"I'm sure you'll do great," he said.

I shrugged. "I know. I'm pretty sure I'll get the part, but it's a big deal."

He chuckled, which was weird because I hadn't said anything funny.

"What?" I asked as we reached the candy counter.

"Hold on," he said, and smiled politely at the girl behind the counter. "Large popcorn and . . ." He turned to me. "Root beer?"

I nodded. He'd known me forever, so it made sense that he knew my favorite drink.

Once the girl left to get our order, he turned back toward me and gave me a look. "No offense, Sitara, but I don't think the Knot's Valley Little Theater is a"—he paused to do air quotes—"'big deal.'"

Seriously? So much for "no offense." "It's a big deal to me, Rohan! It's the start of my live-theater acting career. It all counts, you know."

"Sorry," he said, not looking all that sorry. "I didn't mean it like that. But acting's not exactly a safe career path. You have to admit that being successful at it is a long shot."

I didn't want to admit anything. But I did say, "Well, I'm sorry it's not as safe as *business* or *baking*."

"There's nothing wrong with business. Or baking *as* a business," he said, his back straightening as he frowned down at me. "Your parents' shop does well, and they're well known and respected in the community. That's something to admire. It's what I aspire to."

*I guess you aspire to being boring*, I didn't say. "Whatever" is what I *did* say, sounding a bit pouty even to myself. But did he have to be so practical all the time? Maybe I didn't want to be practical. I was more interested in following my dreams than a *safe* path. "I have dreams, you know, Rohan."

"I'm sorry," he said, this time sounding like he meant it. Maybe because he realized I was starting to get really upset. "I didn't mean to come down on your dreams, Sitara. And you do have a really nice voice. Maybe Preeti can help you somehow. She *is* a big deal."

*Right. But a* Bollywood *big deal, not a Broadway one*, I thought. Still, I guess he had a point. She probably did know a lot of people, maybe even some from Hollywood or Broadway.

We grabbed our snacks and went into the theater, taking seats on the aisle (because the safety-conscious Rohan said it was best to be on the aisle in case of emergency).

While I was still excited to see the movie (and Preeti), Rohan had sucked some of the fun out of the evening.

It didn't help that I knew if I had been there with Hiro, we'd be laughing our faces off and having the best time. *That* was the date I wanted to be on.

Finally, the movie started, and within minutes we were both transported. It was the first time I'd watched one of Preeti's movies since learning that she was moving to the area, and I really noticed her talent; she was a fabulous actress. Not just a fabulous *Bollywood* actress, but a fabulous actress, period. Plus, she had a beautiful singing voice. I began to think that maybe she did Bollywood movies because she liked them and not just because she wasn't good enough to act on Broadway. I'd never thought about Bollywood as someone's first choice. But Preeti made it look so good and obviously took it very seriously.

I wondered if when she was my age, she

looked into her mirror and sang Bollywood songs the way I belted out songs from Broadway shows like *Les Mis* and *Hamilton* (and TWOz, of course). Maybe she did. Maybe being a Bollywood star had been *her* dream.

I was really loving the movie, having forgotten about the stuff with Rohan. That is until about halfway through the film, when there was a really awkward love scene. Actually, it wouldn't have been so awkward if Rohan hadn't been sitting right beside me. But even though I didn't exactly *want* it to be a date, I couldn't help but wonder if it *was* one, just as Preeti and her guy on screen were about to kiss.

*Here it comes!* my brain was telling me. *A big romantic kiss!* My face got so hot, and I hoped Rohan couldn't see me—thankfully it was dark other than the light flickering from the screen. I pulled my hair forward to cover my face, so if he looked over, he wouldn't see me blushing.

I snuck a glance at him through the strands of hair, and he was smiling back at me. Gah!

Then, like in slow motion, his hand lifted out of the popcorn bucket that was balanced between us and drifted over toward me. As I stared at him, he pushed the wall of hair back behind my ear, exposing my paprika-red cheeks.

*What are you doing? Why are you touching me? What does it mean?* I thought, but no words would come out of my mouth. Out of the corner of my eye, Preeti and her hunky guy were making out on the screen, larger than life. Kissing. Right there beside us.

I held my breath, waiting for whatever Rohan was going to do. Because I had no idea. If only Yael was here sitting beside me so she could whisper into my other ear, telling me what was about to happen and what *I* should do.

Rohan looked away from me toward the screen, and his eyes went wide as he seemed to notice the romantic scene in front of him.

I swallowed and turned back to the screen too, wondering what had just happened between us. Is this what they mean when they call it a "moment"? Did it mean this was officially a date?

I absently reached into the popcorn, only to touch something warm, and it wasn't hot, buttery popcorn as I was expecting, but the smooth skin of Rohan's hand. I gasped and looked up at him.

He was smiling at me. This *had* to be another moment. Or maybe a continuation of the same one. I don't know—what do I know about romance and moments and dates with boys?! Exactly nothing!

Then all of a sudden, as I stared at him, wondering if maybe he was going to kiss me and sort of hoping he was, a handful of popcorn kernels came flying at my face.

I blinked several times in surprise. Had he seriously just thrown popcorn at me? During our moment? In the middle of the most romantic scene ever?

Rohan—the most non-jokey guy I knew—had just thrown popcorn at me?

"Why so serious, Sitara?" he whispered as he smirked at me.

Had I been totally wrong? Had I imagined the moment? I hadn't watched a lot of romantic movies, but I was pretty sure none of them had the guy throwing popcorn at the girl instead of kissing her.

I suddenly felt SO stupid. For thinking it had been a moment. For thinking he—Rohan, the guy I'd known forever and who was most definitely NOT Hiro, my crush—had been about to kiss me. For wanting him to.

I dug in the bucket of popcorn and pulled

out a big handful, which I then chucked at him before I stood up. "I have to go to the bathroom," I announced, pushing past him, suddenly glad that we were right on the aisle, because this definitely counted as an emergency.

My fingers hovered over the screen of my phone because I couldn't figure out what to say to Yael. There were so many things whirling around in my head, but how was I supposed to sort it all out in a text? I needed her help, but I didn't have time to tell her everything that had happened so she could analyze it all and tell me what to do. I didn't even know if this was a date!

Then I realized that it was Shabbat, which meant, because she was Jewish, Yael's phone would be off and I'd be getting no help from her. That's when I noticed a text from Desmond that had come in during the movie.

Hey Tara, Hiro told me you were going to come over to rehearse with him, but then said you canceled. You still going to try out for Dorothy? You're SO much better than Meg!

I smiled at that, loving his encouragement and obvious good taste in actors.

Yes, I'm still trying out, I sent him.

You will steal the spotlight! he texted back immediately.

My cheeks warmed up as I thought about how he'd given me the spotlight during drama club. He really was a nice guy.

I was about to respond and thank him when just then a text came from Hiro. I could be at his house right now, rehearsing. Or I could have invited him here to the movie, and we could be out there, not *not* kissing.

Or maybe he would have thrown popcorn at me too.

Hey, U coming over to practice? he asked.

Huh? I'd told him I was coming to see the film and Preeti and that's why I couldn't rehearse with him. Not to mention that Desmond had just said Hiro had told him I wasn't coming, so it's not like he'd forgotten.

At the movie, I sent back, confused.

You should bail. More fun here with me and Meg!

Wait. What? Him *and Meg*?

I just stared at my phone, my heart sinking into my belly. No, lower: into my foot. Had he invited her after I told him I couldn't practice with him? Or had she invited herself? Or maybe he'd invited her when he thought maybe I was coming and it would have been him *and* her and me. I had no idea what was happening, but if I'd ever had a chance with Hiro, I might have ruined it by coming to this movie. With Rohan.

Wait. Oh no! Did Hiro think I was on a date? Wait, how could he? Did he even know I was here with another boy?

Too.

Many.

Questions.

Tears pooled in my eyes as I watched the little dots that said Hiro had more to say. Except, did I even want to see it if he was just going to go on and talk about him and Meg? Not really.

Before his next text came, I sent back: Can't. Need to stay and see movie star. You should come here!

He should come here? What? Why would I even say that? But I knew the answer: Desperation plus panic equals Tara saying stupid things. *Ugh, Tara, what is wrong with you?*

Nope, he returned. Me and Meg are practicing. She's really good 2! You should practice or you'll be stuck playing Toto. Woof! And then he sent a dog emoji.

Like my heart wasn't already broken and in

my shoe? Now it was like he'd drop-kicked it to the other side of the bathroom to get covered in dust and hair and all kinds of gross bathroom things. Why would he say that?!

I have to go, I sent, and then turned off my phone and put it into my purse before I could see any more devastating texts. I wiped away the tears that had escaped, took a few deep breaths, and left the bathroom. I almost called my parents to come and pick me up but didn't want to have to explain why I wasn't leaving with their favorite person in the world.

Instead, I straightened my shoulders, took a few more deep breaths, and strode into the theater. The show must go on.

"Everything okay?" Rohan whispered as I squished past him to my seat.

I nodded and stared at the screen. At least the awkward romantic scene was over.

For both Preeti's character *and* me.

Thank goodness.


"That was so good!" Rohan said as the credits began and the lights came on.

I nodded, happy to pretend that the drama from earlier had never happened.

The crowd in the theater started getting ready to leave when a man came out to the front of the seats with a microphone in his hand.

"Everyone, may I have your attention, please?"

As people settled down, waiting for him to make his announcement, Rohan and I looked at each other knowingly.

The theater guy spoke: "We have a special treat for you all. We have none other than the star of *Masala Madness*, Preeti Chandran, here to say a few words about the film!"

An excited murmur went through the crowd, which suddenly turned into a standing ovation as Preeti came out from a side door. She looked amazing, her diamond nose ring glittering in the overhead spotlight, her makeup dramatic and perfect. I couldn't believe I was in the same room as Preeti! I suddenly understood the meaning of the word "starstruck." She was as beautiful in person as she was on the screen. Preeti strutted with confidence up to the man. She nodded at him as she took the microphone and then, with a broad smile, addressed the excited audience.

"Thank you so much! I'm so honored. Please, please, sit down." She gestured for everyone to take a seat and waited before she went on. "As some of you may know, my fiancé is from this area, so after my wedding, I will be spending a lot of time—when I'm not on set—here in Knot's Valley. Already I feel so welcome here and look forward to becoming a true member of the community."

A roar went up from the crowd; then someone stuck up their hand.

Preeti smiled up at the girl. "Yes?"

"I heard a rumor that you were going to be starting up an acting program for youth at the community center—is that true?"

"Wow, word really travels in small towns, doesn't it?" Preeti said with a chuckle. "There is some truth to that, but it's still in the works. That's all I can say for now."

I actually covered my mouth with my hands like an emoji for "shocked." A local acting class founded by Preeti Chandran! Rohan was shaking my shoulders and laughing while a chorus of "Yesssss!" erupted around me.

Preeti continued. "I just have to get through my wedding first. Acting like a cool and calm bride is probably my most difficult role to date," she said, making everyone laugh.

Rohan turned toward me. "Speaking of

weddings," he said quietly, "you're going to hers, right?"

I opened my mouth, but nothing came out. Her wedding was at the same time as the TWOz auditions.

"Sitara," Rohan said, frowning at me because he must have clued in to my indecision. "You have to go. Not only will it help your parents, but it's *Preeti*. And she's going to be helping local kids with acting. That's exactly what you want, isn't it?"

Not *exactly* what I wanted. But maybe I'd been too quick to dismiss Bollywood. It seemed cheesy compared to Broadway. But Preeti was anything but cheesy. She was graceful and polished and sophisticated and . . . Was Bollywood what I wanted for me?

"Yes, but . . . the auditions . . ."

Rohan shook his head as Preeti answered more questions from the audience about the movie.

I felt bad, but I really wanted to be in the play. Not just that, but I wanted to beat out Meg to be Dorothy. I couldn't let her think I was bailing on the auditions. I also didn't want Hiro to think I didn't like him anymore either.

But as I watched Preeti at the front of the

theater, I wished there was a way to audition *and* attend her wedding.

As Preeti finished speaking and we all gave her another standing ovation, I was still no closer to deciding. I had less than a week to make up my mind.

What should I do?

---

*Tara goes to the audition. Turn to page 137.*
*Tara goes to the wedding. Turn to page 88.*

137

88

# Supporting Actors

I couldn't believe I was at Preeti and Sanjit's big, flashy wedding! The one that everyone in town—everyone who loved Bollywood—was talking about. Sure, maybe I wasn't at the ceremony, but everyone knows the party *after* the ceremony is the best part of weddings.

The rooms at the hotel where it was being held had been sold out for weeks, and as we'd pulled our catering van in, we saw a huge lineup of limousines in the half-circle driveway. Limousines mean celebrities, and I could not wait to see who was in our little town to help

Preeti and Sanjit celebrate their big day.

Especially since we weren't just there to bring the food: Preeti herself had invited the four of us—Mom, Dad, Rohan, and me—to be her special guests at the wedding reception, too! I'd been practicing my bhangra dance moves all week.

But before we could join the party, we had work to do. While the ceremony was still going on in another room, Rohan and I were busy in the reception hall, setting up the sweet table. We arranged everything carefully on the gigantic silver platters that were built up on gold fabric-covered tiers. My mandala cookies (which I did not complain about decorating, because they were for PREETI CHANDRAN'S WEDDING) were arranged around the bottom, then came the sugary samosas, and then on top were all our special laddus, jalebis, and barfis (which, trust me, are a lot better than they sound!).

While we were setting those up, the hotel's caterers were setting up the zillions of hot food stations, and my parents were putting the final touches on the wedding cake, which took up its own table because, obviously, it was a VBD.

Dad had totally outdone himself, creating

a layered, toasted-coconut-flavored cake that looked like it had an embroidered scarf (matching Preeti's stunning red wedding sari) draped over it. The "scarf" was made of fondant with icing rosettes, edible beads, and even real gold leaf. It was a piece of art that was almost too beautiful to eat. Almost.

I had gotten tears in my eyes when I'd first seen it and was so proud of my dad. Preeti was going to love it when she saw it, because *anyone* would be lucky to have a stunning cake like that at her wedding.

Not two minutes after we finished setting up and making everything look perfect, we knew the wedding party was coming when we heard the roar of the big crowd out in the hall getting louder and louder.

The servers came forward with platters of champagne and sparkling juice, ready to greet the guests and the just-married couple.

I looked down at my new outfit—an emerald-green-and-gold sari—to make sure it was arranged properly and that I hadn't spilled anything on it. When I'd gone shopping with my mom for the occasion, I had planned to buy a western-style party dress, but when we got to the mall and started looking, I realized that for Preeti's block-buster wedding, a traditional sari was the right choice.

I was right, too; I'd worn a lot of costumes and makeup in my thirteen years, but I'd never felt prettier or more confident than I did in that moment.

As I lifted my eyes to see the crowd enter the ballroom, I heard Rohan say my name.

He was smiling like crazy. "What?" I asked, but I could sort of guess what he was thinking.

"You look so nice, Sitara."

"It's new," I said, running my hands down the front of the outfit, admiring the vibrant fabric, and appreciating Rohan's compliment. He was much smoother than Hiro.

"It's not the sari," he said. "It's *you*."

*Oh.* When I lifted my gaze again, he was staring into my eyes. That totally felt like a *date* thing to say.

Then, before I could tell him he looked hand-some (because he did), the doors swung open and in came all the guests.

I didn't see Preeti and Sanjit, but once all the guests were in the room, the DJ asked everyone to take their seats.

A few minutes later drumming began out in the hallway. "What's happening?" I asked. Rohan just shrugged, and as he did, I noticed we'd moved closer together, his shoulder brushing against mine.

The drums got louder as the two men playing them came into the room and moved over beside the DJ's table. After what felt like a forever of excitement and anticipation, though it was probably only a couple of minutes, the DJ started up the music to go along with the drums. A second later Preeti and Sanjit came into the room amid hoots, hollers, and applause as all the guests jumped to their feet. The couple, who were holding hands, glided together into the middle of the dance floor as though they'd planned it (which they probably had).

They turned to face each other, did a little nod, and then, at the exact same moment, broke into a famous dance from *Love on the Maharajas' Express*, Preeti's most popular film.

The roar of the guests got even louder, and even Rohan and I joined in, shouting and clapping at the couple in encouragement.

A few minutes into the dance, they faced each other and did another nod before they turned to the crowd and gestured at everyone to join them on the dance floor.

Not hesitating for even a second—because of course I wanted to dance and had been practicing for this moment—I ran out there and joined them as we all fell into step, imitating the moves they'd been doing when it was just the two of them. Several minutes later I happened to glance up and saw Rohan standing by the side of the dance floor, watching. He was smiling and tapping a foot to the music, but what was up with that? This was our music! Why wasn't he dancing?

Preeti must have had the same thought, breaking away from Sanjit to dance up to Rohan, beckoning him out onto the floor. He shook his head no, but she put one hand behind her head and another on her hip like she was telling him with her movements that he needed to get his butt on the floor. He must have understood, and while he didn't look really happy about it, he joined the dancing crowd.

Rohan tried to follow along, but he wasn't a great dancer and was so stiff, like his joints were rusty. But he did try and looked like he was having fun, which was what mattered.

I looked over at the bride and was surprised

to see her smiling at me. Then she nodded toward Rohan and gave me a wink. Was she was telling me to go for him? *What?!* When I looked back at him, he was concentrating on his feet and hadn't seen. Thank goodness!

Once it was time for dinner, I escaped to the bathroom to catch my breath and fix my hair, because once dinner started, I was probably going to have to eat quickly and then take my place at the sweet table.

Also, I wanted to check my phone, because Yael was at the auditions for TWOz.

I felt some regret over not going to the auditions because I knew I would have given it my all. It would have felt so glorious to have gotten the part. But while I was sad about missing the chance to play Dorothy, I knew that assisting my parents at the wedding was the right thing to do. Not only would it help them to realize their dream, but it would be a good step toward realizing mine, too. Preeti was my Glinda—I was sure of it. It was important to me that she not just like me (though that was REALLY IMPORTANT) but also see that I was hardworking and committed.

Of course, it wasn't *all* work; I *was* having a good time. And like Rohan had said, there would be more productions down the road, and I had Bollywood Boot Camp to look forward to! Plus, Preeti would only have one wedding, and it had been crazy fun so far, AND I was getting to show off my dancing skills!

Also, thinking about Hiro at the audition, I was glad not to be so caught up in him anymore. He still thought it was hilarious to bark at me and call me Toto. I couldn't even remember why I'd thought he was so great. He was so immature. Maybe I hadn't noticed because his goofing around had seemed fun before. But plenty of other boys were just as handsome, way more mature, and a lot smarter. Especially older boys. Even ones who weren't the best dancers.

I opened up a text that had come in from Yael: Audition Update-Hiro got Scarecrow part, but Meg choked and is stuck being a flying monkey! She added a bunch of emojis—monkeys, shocked faces, and, of course, a string of poop ones.

I texted back: Flying monkey? Srsly? HA! Although I was a teeny tiny bit jealous that she had a part at all. But only the teeniest tiniest bit, because no one wants to be a flying monkey.

Right? she sent back. Hiro laughed at her. Kind of mean. Don't think she likes him anymre.

So that was interesting.

Won't be as fun without you, she sent with a frowny face.

I'll still go to the show to see ur awsme sets! And Meg the monky!

She sent a thumbs-up, and I told her I had to go.

I noticed a text from Desmond: Too bad you couldn't come to auditions. U would have made a great Dorothy. Hpe ur having fun at the wedding! C U Monday @ school.

I smiled at his message. Even though he seemed a little shy and dorky sometimes, Paloma was right—he really was the sweetest guy. I was about to respond when the bathroom door squeaked open. I saw it was Preeti, so I sent him a quick gtg and a thumbs-up and tucked my phone away.

"There you are, Sitara!" Preeti said, gliding over to me and holding out both her hands for me to take.

As I placed my hands in hers, I was able to see the full effect of the henna designs on her hands, the kind every Indian bride wore for her wedding.

"Oh, Preeti! Your *mehndi* are so beautiful."

"Thank you," she said with a gracious smile. "But I didn't come find you to show off."

If *I* had such beautiful designs on my hands, I would have totally done some showing off, but then I realized what she'd said and raised my eyebrows at her. "You came to find me on purpose?"

She let go of my hands and nodded toward the mirror. "Well, to fix my lipstick, too, but I wanted to talk to you."

I inhaled sharply. "Is there something wrong with the cookies?"

She smiled and shook her head. "No, nothing like that. Your cookies are perfect. Your . . . *friend* Rohan told me that you missed out on an important audition to be here tonight."

Grrr, Rohan! I hadn't wanted Preeti to know. "Oh, it's okay. It was just for a local production of *The Wizard of Oz*," I said, waving her off so she wouldn't think it was a VBD.

"And you were, of course, going to try out for the lead?"

I nodded, because why would I want anything *other* than the lead? I thought about Meg stuck being a flying monkey and had to fight off a shiver.

"Well," she said, leaning back against the counter and crossing her ankles. "Of course I want you in my Bollywood Acting Boot Camp, but what would you say to some private tutoring from my own voice and acting coach? Would that help make up for it?"

I probably looked like a fish out of water with the way I was gaping my mouth at her until I could finally say, "What? Preeti, no . . . You don't have to make up for anything! I'm having a great time!"

She shrugged. "Nonetheless . . . I like you, and Rohan didn't just tell me that you missed your audition. He told me you're very talented, too, and that you would have gotten the part."

As I processed this, she pulled a lipstick from a hidden pocket and then turned toward the mirror to reapply it. "You know, you remind me of myself at your age. I'd hate to see that talent go to waste." She caught my eye in the mirror. "Unless you don't want the tutoring?"

"No! I mean, yes, I do! Very much. But are you sure you—" I stopped because she gave me a look that clearly said that she *was* sure. Very sure. And that I should stop questioning. "Thank you, Preeti. I would really love that. Thank you so much!" I launched forward and threw my arms around her.

She laughed and gave me a squeeze before letting me go. "You can thank your . . . *friend*. He's really sweet, by the way." She turned back to the mirror and pressed her freshly painted lips together. "He likes you. You know that, don't you?"

"Ummm . . ."

She clearly thought Rohan was *more* than a friend.

After everything that had happened between us, did I want him to be?

She laughed and then turned away from the mirror to look at me and tapped my nose with her finger. "Yes, you do know. You're cute together."

What was I supposed to say to that? "Shouldn't you be out there?" I asked, changing the subject and pointing at the door. "It's your wedding day!"

"Yes, it is. And I'm so happy, which means I want everyone to be happy! You're right, though; I do need to get out there. But once my honeymoon is over, and we settle in, my acting coach will be staying with us for a while, helping me rehearse for my next film. In between my own sessions, you'll be able to take private lessons. How does that sound?"

Um, amazing? There was only one problem. "Preeti, I . . . I don't think my parents will want to . . . I mean, your coach is probably really expensive."

Preeti smiled and reached for the door. "Good thing she takes payment in samosas, then, huh?" Before I could say anything, she gave me a mischievous smile and left the bathroom.

I returned to the ballroom and found my seat at the kids' table (not the baby kids, but all the kids my age, which was a relief) next to Rohan.

"Preeti's voice and acting coach!" I blurted out.

"Huh?"

I couldn't help but bounce in my seat and clap my hands. "I'm going to get private lessons! Do you believe it?"

"Yes," he said with a chuckle. "Of course I do. I told her how good you are, so she asked me if I thought it would be a good idea."

I wanted to hug him, but it seemed weird. Oh, who cares?! I threw my arms around him for a quick hug. "Thank you so much, Rohan! I am so excited I can't even!"

When I pulled back, his face was as scarlet as Preeti's dress, and he looked suddenly very shy, but it was cute. Really cute. Like, boyfriend cute.

"You deserve it," he said. "Bollywood, Broadway, Hollywood—whatever you want. You're going to be a star someday, Sitara."

It was the nicest thing anyone had ever said to me, and it took my breath away.

Just then the DJ called out that dinner was served, and the ballroom was filled with the sounds of chairs scraping the floor as everyone got up to rush over to the different food stations—us included, because dancing is hungry work!

With Rohan right beside me, I followed my nose over to where the rich aromas of butter chicken, chana masala, and shrimp biryani were coming from, my mouth watering like crazy. Except a bunch of people beat us to it, so we grabbed plates and got in line.

"So," Rohan began. "When do you start the lessons?"

I shrugged. "Not sure. After their honeymoon, so I guess a few weeks."

"Right . . . so . . . uh . . . I mean, if you're not busy and you don't have rehearsals, I guess, um . . ."

"Rohan?" I said, losing my patience with all the hesitating, especially if he was trying to say what I thought he was. "Are you trying to ask me out?"

He shifted his weight from one foot to the other and began to stammer again but then blew out a breath and said, "Yes, Sitara. I guess I am."

"Well," I said as we shuffled forward in the line. "I would be up for seeing *Masala Madness* next weekend."

A grin spread across his face. "Really?"

I shrugged. "Sure. You know me—I love my Bollywood movies. I can watch them again and again, especially the ones with Preeti in them." I looked past him to where my mom was by the kitchen door, focused on us. Her hands were clasped together, and she looked happier than the bride. I resisted the urge to roll my eyes at her, but seriously, could she be any more obvious?

Rohan didn't seem to notice and leaned his shoulder into mine. "Awesome. It's a date."

I beamed a smile over at him; it was nice to know for sure.

# A Surprise Cameo

I was halfway to Hiro's house when I got a text from Rohan. My heart thumped hard as I read it. Still time to come to the movie.

Was he trying to get me to bail on Hiro and go to the movie with him because he thought of it as a date? Going to the movies was definitely a date activity, but it was Rohan—did he think of me that way? It was so confusing. I put my phone away to focus on getting to Hiro's place. Which meant I just got more and more nervous about going to my crush's house.

I had so many questions whirling around in

my head: Would his mom be home? How about his siblings? I wasn't even sure if he *had* siblings, but if he did, I hoped they didn't get in the way, because there was a good chance that him inviting me over was a date. And it wasn't just me who thought so either; when I'd asked my friends, Yael and Gemma thought it was definitely a date. Paloma was undecided, but even still, that was three against one, so it was probably a date, like, I was 90 percent sure.

As I walked down the street, I could tell by the house numbers that I was getting close. He lived at number 127, and I was already at 123. This was about to happen! It was a huge VBD, and I was nervous AND excited. Like, NERVCITED!

Then I heard my name. I looked toward what had to be Hiro's house, but there was no one there.

"Over here," the voice said, drawing my attention toward 125.

There was a guy standing in the open front doorway. I recognized him right away. "Desmond?"

He seemed confused to see me, which made two of us. "Yeah. What are you doing here?"

I did a double take and asked, "What am *I*

doing here?" I looked from him over to the house next door and back. That's when it clicked into place that he wasn't at Hiro's house but standing in the doorway of 125 like he owned it. "Wait, do you live here?"

He nodded.

Ah, it all made sense now.

"I'm going to rehearse with Hiro." I pointed at the house next to his to show that Hiro lived there. Then I felt stupid because of course he knew that.

"Oh . . . cool," he said, frowning. He'd seemed so friendly in the caf. Now he was back to his weird, quiet self.

"Yeah. We're going to practice for next weekend's auditions."

"You're going to do great," he suddenly blurted with a smile. And now he was friendly again. But then he looked down at his shoes.

"Thanks," I said.

"What have you got there?" he asked, nodding toward the bag in my hand. The one I'd forgotten about.

"Just some sweets from my family's shop." *For Hiro,* I thought.

"Oh," he said, staring at the bag like he hadn't eaten in *days.*

I swallowed an impatient sigh. "Want to try one?"

He jogged down his front steps. "Sure. Thanks."

"What are you doing out here, anyway?"

He looked up at me, his cheeks suddenly getting a lot pinker. "Oh, I was just, um, checking the mailbox."

"On Friday night?" I asked. "After dinner?"

After several long seconds of him staring at me blankly, he said, "For flyers. We get a lot of flyers and junk mail."

That seemed weird, but whatever. I opened the bag and held it toward him. "You can have *one* thing." I'd brought lots for Hiro to choose from, but they were for him, not his nice but dorky next-door neighbor.

Desmond reached his hand into the bag. "Don't touch them all," I blurted, then realized I was being rude and felt my face heat.

"I won't," he assured me, not seeming to notice my awkwardness as he grabbed a treat. "Oh, a jalebi—I love these! Thanks, Tara."

"You're welcome." It impressed me that he knew what it was. "Well, I'd better go."

He nodded and took a bite of his jalebi when

a woman, who I assumed was his mom, popped her head out the front door. "Desmond! What are you doing? One second you're vacuuming the living room and then—oh, hello," she said as she noticed me.

Huh? He'd said he was checking the mailbox. I glanced over at the house and noticed the big picture window. Through it I could see the long handle of a vacuum sticking up.

He cleared his throat and said, "Mom, this is Tara Singh. She's in my class; her parents own Mmmumbai."

Mrs. Flynn's eyes lit up. "Oh, I love that place! I get those maple syrup laddus for my book club meetings."

"Nice to meet you," I said, feeling like I should now offer *her* something from my bag too. When I did, she thanked me but waved me off. Thank goodness.

"Anyway," I said to Desmond. "I'd better get going."

"Right," he said. "Anyway, see you at school."

He went back inside the house, without even looking at the mailbox. I knew it! He'd totally come out to talk to me when he'd seen me walking by.

Hmm.

He also knew about my family's shop.

And what a jalebi is.

Hmm.

The mysterious Desmond Flynn.

By the time I arrived at 127, I was so sweaty from nerves I felt like I'd been dipped in maple syrup. Once I'd left Desmond and walked across the lawn to Hiro's place, questions flooded my brain: Would he like the treats I'd brought? Would we rehearse for real, or would he want to do something else, like play video games or . . . ?

And the most important question of all: Was this a date?

The door opened to reveal a smiling lady. "Hi," she said, opening the door wider and gesturing me inside. "You must be Tara. Come on in. I'm Rumi, Hiro's mom."

Did it mean anything that she already knew my name and was expecting me? "Nice to meet you," I said, just like I had with Desmond's mom. Apparently, it was meet-everyone's-mom day.

"They're in the basement," Mrs. Nakahara said. "I'll show you to the stairs. Can I get you something to drink?"

Wait. Had she said *they're* in the basement?

Hiro's mom stood there, staring at me, when I realized she was waiting for an answer. I rewound the film in my head. "Oh, uh, no thanks," I said. "I'm fine. I'll just go find Hiro aaaaaaand . . ."

She didn't finish my sentence for me, instead leading me to a door off the kitchen. She opened it and waved toward the stairs. She had no idea the turmoil I felt over not knowing who was downstairs. "Send Hiro up for drinks soon—I know acting and singing can be thirsty work!"

And then there was nothing to do but go down the steps, scared of what I was about to encounter because I suddenly had a funny feeling that this *wasn't* a date and that Hiro had invited someone else to come practice and of course that someone was—

"Meg!" said Hiro as I started down the stairs. "You crushed that scene!"

Ugh. I wanted to crush Hiro. Or at least run out of his house before he could even see me, but what would I say to his mother?

I was stuck.

I took a deep breath and headed the rest of the way down the stairs.

They were standing in the middle of the

basement across from each other, each with a script in their hand. At least they were rehearsing and not down here kissing or something, so *that* was a relief. Though the way Meg was looking at him made it clear she was kissing him in her head.

I scowled.

But then I thought of Preeti and how she had the acting career *and* the guy and she probably *never* scowled. I cleared my throat, pasted a smile on my face, and said a very happy "Hey, guys!" I was an actress, after all.

They both turned and looked at me: Hiro with his bright grin and Meg with her narrowed eyes that proved Hiro hadn't given her the full cast list for today's rehearsal either. Even though I'd only found out two seconds before, it felt good that she didn't have the opportunity to see *my* surprise.

"Toto! Woof!" Hiro said, and Meg chuckled.

"It's *Tara*," I corrected, getting a little tired of the whole Toto thing. Would he ever let it go?

He didn't exactly clue in. "We're so glad you came!"

Meg gave him a snarly glance that I was pretty sure meant *Speak for yourself!*

"Me too," I lied because I was *not* so glad if

it meant he was going to bark at me. "I brought some snacks, too."

Hiro took the bag from me and looked inside. "Cool. We can have these after we run some lines. Unless you want to practice singing first?"

I shrugged. "Whatever you want."

He smiled. "Okay, let's go through the audition scene again. I'll be the Scarecrow, obviously, Meg, you be the Tin Man, and, Tara, you can be Dorothy."

"How come *she* gets to be Dorothy?" Meg demanded.

Hiro gave her a confused look. "Because you were Dorothy a minute ago and since either one of you might get the role, it's smart for me to practice with both of you. I have to be flexible."

Ugh. Did he realize how dumb and horrible that sounded? I felt Meg's angry stare on me but didn't look at her because sudden tears had pooled in my eyes and I did not want her to see. In fact, I wasn't sure I wanted to look at Hiro just then either. I pulled the folded-up script out of my pocket. "Let's just get started," I muttered.

We practiced for a long time, and after a while I forgot to be competitive with Meg and, in fact, told her her timing was spot on. My compliment threw her off her next line, which made me really want to snicker, but I composed myself, proud of my maturity.

"Would you like to practice the scene where she sees Auntie Em in the crystal ball?" Meg asked.

Everyone who is familiar with the musical knows this is a great scene for showing off dramatic range. I stood up while Meg settled on the couch, and we smiled at each other as we set up the scene. Like, *really* smiled.

It actually all seemed okay . . . until we broke for a snack and Hiro went upstairs to get some drinks.

"I'm going to be Dorothy," Meg said, going back to her snarky self, the one I was more used to than the nice, helpful person she'd been the last hour. "You can be one of the witches if you want, but *I'm* Dorothy."

Yeah, like *that* was happening. "You'll have to beat me out first," I said, matching her snarky tone with my own. "Good luck with that."

She gave me a look as though to say, *Oh, it is on.*

Whatever. A tiny part of me didn't like that I had to audition against her, because usually she was pretty good, but most of me was confident that she could never out-act me, no matter how much she wanted me to think she could.

"Hiro too," she said, though in a lower tone as she glanced toward the stairs.

"Hiro too, what?" I said.

"He's going to be my boyfriend. I bet he didn't even invite you here tonight. You probably heard him telling me and invited yourself."

Uh, not quite. In fact, if I'd known he'd asked her over, I probably wouldn't even have come. Especially since I didn't know what it meant that he'd invited both of us. Did that mean he liked both of us but couldn't decide? I needed to talk to Yael to get some best friend advice. Desperately.

"Whatever, Meg," I said, and went into the bathroom off the rec room. I pulled out my phone to text Yael and tell her that Hiro had also invited Meg over to practice.

I waited for her response, except then I realized it was Friday night, and, while her family wasn't super religious, her parents made her power down her electronics for Shabbat. That meant I'd have to wait until the next night to hear from her. I was going to try Gemma or Paloma, but they didn't know the whole situation, and I didn't have enough time to explain it over text.

I was on my own, at least until tomorrow night, so I was putting my phone away when I got a text from Rohan. I thought he was about to make me feel bad again for not going to the movie with him (a decision I was regretting—thank you, Meg Hamilton) when I noticed Preeti's name in his message. That made me read the whole thing: Movie was awsm! Preeti is starting up a Bollywood acting boot camp 4 kids. Perfect for u!

Wow. Preeti may not know Broadway, but she was still a real actress—a successful and talented one—and I could learn a lot from her.

I sent Rohan a text back with some excited emojis and a ton of exclamation points.

You're coming to help out at her wedding, too, right?

I was about to tell him yes but then remembered her wedding was the same time as the TWOz auditions. I hated that both events were the same night—so unfair! As I was thinking about it and how I wished I had a time machine so I could be in two places at once, Rohan sent another text: Your parents have been telling her about your acting, and she invited us as guests and even said she can't wait to see you act!

OMG! I sent back. *Preeti Chandran* wanted to

see *me* act?! Small-town Sitara Singh? But now what was I supposed to do?

I didn't want to miss out on the auditions. Winning the role would be the beginning of my yellow brick road to stardom. The whole town went to shows at the Knot's Valley Little Theater, and the arts reporter from the city *always* reviewed their productions.

Plus, there was Hiro.

Except . . . *did* I like him? I'd had a crush on him forever, but now that I was at his house, he was acting like a jerk—barking at me and making it seem as though he liked Meg.

Amid all that noise I suddenly remembered the sound of Desmond's soft voice saying my name.

Rohan sent another text. Well? Can I tell her you'll be at the wedding?

I had to make up my mind. Would I go to the audition and try out for Dorothy, or skip it and go to Preeti's wedding?

---

*Tara goes to the audition. Turn to page 116.*
*Tara goes to the wedding. Turn to page 88.*

# The Spotlight

"Nailed it!" Hiro shouted, and without warning jumped up out of his aisle seat to give the girl who'd just auditioned a big high five as she walked past him.

"Uh, did he not see what she just did?" I whispered into Yael's left ear. We were sitting in the Knot's Valley Little Theater in the third row, amid the million kids trying out. I had yet to go up for my audition and was SUPER nervous.

I was also getting SUPER excited. Especially if this girl, who had most definitely *not* just nailed her audition, was what I was up against.

"Right?" Yael whispered back. "So far you've got nothing to worry about."

Hiro was grinning at the girl—Carly Somethingorother. She'd announced she was from the next town over, so it was weird that Hiro was acting like they were besties. Did he even know her? She smiled at him as she took her seat.

Hiro dropped down into the empty seat beside me. Even though he had chosen the chair right next to mine, I was hit with a pang of jealousy because I wanted him to only high-five *me* and tell me *I* nailed it, not some random other girl!

A tiny part of me liked him even more for being such a nice guy, but the rest of me wanted to put him in a hot-air balloon and take him with me to a land far, far away where there was no Carly Whatshername, or, more importantly—

"Megan Hamilton," the guy with the clipboard called out.

Meg jumped out of her seat. "Here!"

"Go on up and tell us a bit about yourself," Jen, the casting director, said with a wave of her hand toward the stage.

Meg headed up the small flight of stairs (not tripping at all, not that I'd wanted her to or anything) and took her place onstage, clearing her throat before she pasted a smile on her face. "Um, hi. So I'm Megan—Meg—Hamilton, like the musical *Hamilton*, ha-ha." She paused, but no one laughed since her joke wasn't even remotely funny. Yikes. She cleared her throat, wrung her hands a few times, and then, just before she opened her mouth to speak again, seemed to notice me. Then she narrowed her eyes at me and said, "*I'm* auditioning for the part of Dorothy." It was like she was saying it right to me, as though she were daring me to beat her.

*Challenge accepted,* I thought, narrowing my eyes right back at her.

Hiro clapped and whistled at Meg. I gave him a look, and he shrugged but thankfully stopped applauding.

"Have you done any acting before?" Jen asked Meg.

Meg shifted her weight and unclasped her hands, shaking them out at her sides. "Not professional acting, but I'm in drama club at Knot's Valley Middle. I've been practicing really hard, and I know I'll make *the best* Dorothy."

Of course she was looking at me when she said "the best Dorothy." Right.

"Okay, great," clipboard guy said. "Let's start with the song, and then you can read a page wiiiiiith . . ." He looked down at his clipboard.

*Anyone but Hiro, anyone but Hiro,* I chanted in my head. *Please, please, PLEASE, anyone BUT Hiro.*

"Hiro Nakahara."

Hiro grinned.

I looked at Yael and rolled my eyes as if to say, *Figures.* And she shook her head as if to say, *I know, right?*

The lady at the piano played the intro to "Over the Rainbow," and then Meg started to sing.

Of course I'd heard her before, but today she sounded a lot stronger and more confident than she normally did. "She's really been practicing," I whispered to Yael as I wiped my sweaty palms on the legs of my jeans. Carly Whateverhername was no competition, but unbelievably, Meg Hamilton definitely was.

I took a deep breath and swept my eyes around the theater when I noticed Desmond sitting on his own in the row behind us, about six seats over. He must have felt my eyes on him, because he suddenly looked at me and smiled. Then he mouthed, "Break a leg!" which was nice, so I nodded at him in thanks.

"He's pretty cute, right?" Yael said in my ear.

I turned back toward her. "Who?"

"Duh, *Des*?"

I nodded. "Oh, yeah. You should totally go for him," I said encouragingly.

"Tara, I didn't say that because *I* like him. I think he'd be good for *you*."

Was she serious? I frowned. "Get real, Yael. He's a tech nerd. Not my type. I need an actor, like . . ." I tipped my head slightly toward My Forever Crush on the other side of me.

She shrugged. "I think Des is nice. *And* I think he likes you. He didn't tell *Meg* to break a leg, you know."

I slowly glanced over my shoulder at Desmond again.

Gah! He was looking at me! I quickly turned forward, willing myself not to be embarrassed at being caught looking. I had no reason to be embarrassed, especially since *he'd* been looking too. That canceled out *my* embarrassment. Didn't it?

Meg held the last note of the song, and everyone clapped automatically, except for clipboard guy, who thanked her and gestured for Hiro to come up to read lines with her.

"Break a leg," I said to him as he rose.

He smiled at me and then skipped up onstage, doing his boneless walk over to pick up the page of script from clipboard guy. Everyone laughed at how he was already acting like the Scarecrow. I could even imagine him in a ratty hat and old clothes with straw poking out.

He and Meg started to read the scene together, and from the first lines, they sounded good. Really good.

I hated that they were doing such a great job. I mean, I liked that *Hiro* was, but did he have to do such a great job *with Meg*? Like, did he have to make her look so awesome? Like they belonged onstage together?

As I watched them, I started to get nervous about my own performance and even scared that I wasn't going to be good enough to get the Dorothy part. Had I practiced enough? Was I kidding myself by even being here? I mean, I had always felt pretty good about my acting and singing skills, but could I really beat out Meg? She was owning that stage.

And she and Hiro were effortless together.

Finally, their reading was over, and clipboard guy thanked Meg and asked Hiro to stay onstage so he could do the singing part of his own audition.

Before Hiro let her leave the stage, though, he gave Meg one of his high fives and a winning smile to go along with his "Crushed it, Meg!"

"Ugh, does he need to congratulate everyone like they're the best?" Yael whispered, echoing my own thoughts.

"I know," I said. "His stupid encouragement is making me want to barf." And then I mimed a big fake gag, making Yael laugh.

A moment later, after he did his own intro, Hiro started singing "If I Only Had a Brain," complete with his goofy, but absolutely perfect, Scarecrow dance. He totally killed it, as I knew he would, and I couldn't help but jump to my feet to applaud once he was finished. He was going to get the part—no doubt about it.

So that was *half* my dream cast nailed down.

"Thanks, Hiro," Jen said. "Can you stay onstage to help with reading for . . ."

*Please be me, please be me, PLEEEEEAAAAASE BEEEEEE MEEEEE!*

"Tara Singh."

Finally!

"Break a leg!" Yael said as I popped up out of my seat.

I also heard "Go Tara!" from behind and

about six seats over. I smiled over my shoulder at Desmond, taking his encouragement with me up onto the stage.

I introduced myself quickly, and then we took our places to perform the scene where Dorothy and the Scarecrow meet.

Hiro stood near center stage with his arms out like he was up on a post, and I went to the right side, near the wings.

Once Jen gave us the nod to start, I began to skip down the imaginary yellow brick road. "Follow the yellow brick—oh no!" I exclaimed in my clear theater voice as the "road" ended in front of me. "*Now* where do I go?"

"This way is very nice," the Scarecrow said, pointing to his right.

As we performed the scene, we really got into the rhythm of the dialogue and both loosened up (well, the Scarecrow was already loose; he was made of straw—and Hiro's confidence—after all). I didn't think about the audience or Jen or even the fact that I was acting with Hiro. I was just Dorothy, and it felt awesome.

Once we were finished and took our bows, Hiro gave me one of his huge grins and the expected high five. "Awesome!" he said. "Rocked it!"

"Yeah we did!" I said back.

"Thank you, Hiro," Jen said from the audience. "Why don't you take your seat and let Tara finish her audition."

He did his Scarecrow dance all the way down the stairs, making it seem like he was almost tripping, making everyone laugh. It was funny, but I wished he hadn't done it just then—this was *my* audition, *my* turn to shine; he'd already had his chance.

Once he was off the stage, it was time to sing. I took a few deep breaths in through my nose and out my mouth (as we'd learned in drama club) while the piano lady played the opening bars of "Over the Rainbow." I visualized myself in costume onstage, complete with my hair in braids and wearing my gingham dress, and at the exact right moment, I opened my mouth and began to sing.

It might sound conceited to say, but whatever: I didn't just nail it—I hammered it, pulled it apart, and nailed it back together again.

Once I was done, I looked out at the audience and saw smiles on the faces of both Jen and clipboard guy and knew the part was mine. I also couldn't miss that Hiro had jumped to his feet in his own one-guy standing ovation.

I glanced over at Yael, who was clapping but rolling her eyes toward Hiro at the same time.

"Thank you, Tara," Jen said. "You can take your seat."

I thanked the piano player and returned to the audience.

"Great job, Toto!" Hiro said, giving me another high five as I pushed past him to take my spot between him and Yael. Seriously? He was *still* calling me Toto?

Yael pulled me into a big hug, saying into my ear, "You were amazing up there! I'm so excited for you!" Over her shoulder, I saw Desmond nodding as he stood up and started making his way down the aisle toward me.

I let go of Yael and tugged at my skirt (blue gingham, of course, borrowed from my old Halloween costume, because it couldn't hurt to look the part—acting's all about committing, after all).

"Great job, Tara," Desmond said with a big smile, his blue eyes sparkling at me. Too bad he was almost always looking down. His eyes were stunning.

"Hey, man, didn't see you were here," Hiro said, high-fiving Desmond. Did he high-five *everyone*? It was getting annoying.

Desmond said, "I just wanted to see Tara's audition."

I glanced over at Yael, who waggled her eyebrows at me.

"Anyway," Desmond said quietly. "I'd better go. Just wanted to say you did a really good job."

"Thanks," I said, and watched him go toward the back of the theater, suddenly seeing him in a new light. Yael was right: He was cute. And nice, too. Was she also right when she said he liked me?

"I can't wait to hear the results," Hiro said, drawing my attention back to him.

"I know," I said. "Me too. But you're definitely going to be the Scarecrow."

"You think?" he said, but I could tell by his smile that he knew he was a shoo-in.

"For sure."

He smiled as I looked at him and waited for him to tell me that I was a shoo-in for Dorothy.

And waited.

Then waited some more. Until he nodded and then looked back at the stage, where there was some guy trying out for the Tin Man.

I was going to have to work for it. "It would be so cool if we *both* got the parts we want, right?"

He looked over at me, a dopey grin on his

face. "I guess. I mean, I'm good enough that I can play opposite anyone. But yeah, sure. That would be cool."

Yael seemed to choke on something beside me. It might have been my heart, which seemed to have popped right out of my chest.

"What?" I squeaked.

Hiro shrugged and smiled at me. "You were pretty good, though."

Not exactly the encouragement I'd been hoping for. Or expecting. I mean, I thought . . . I guess I'd thought he wanted to act with me. That maybe he was even into me. He'd specifically told me to meet him at drama club that day when we found out about the production. I'd thought (hoped) that meant he liked me.

Now I wasn't so sure. I looked at Yael, but she shrugged. We'd have to analyze this all later.

I sat back in my seat, suddenly hoping there weren't too many more auditions to go. I couldn't get out of here until nine, when Yael's parents were picking us up to take us to her house. Since my parents were busy at Preeti's wedding, I'd arranged to sleep over at the Lewises'.

As I sat there, watching two kids woodenly run lines onstage, I thought about my parents and Preeti. Then I remembered what Rohan had said when I told him I wasn't going to the wedding: "Then make it worth it. Do your best. Make your dreams come true." I glanced at Hiro and wondered how many dreams would come true tonight.

I wished there had been a way to do the audition *and* help out at the wedding.

Finally, the auditions were over. Jen told us to take a break and they'd have the cast list in a half hour. Thankfully, just down the street was a Dairy Bar, which worked out perfectly, because I felt like I could use some butterscotch sundae therapy.

"Want to come get some ice cream with us?" I said to Hiro.

He looked at me, and I was sure he was going to say yes, but then he looked over at Meg, who was about to walk past us down the aisle. "Uh, I'd like to, but I promised Meg I'd hang out with her. Right, Meg?"

Meg stopped in her tracks, gave him a confused look, and then glanced at me before saying, "Oh yeah, right, of course."

Then she smirked, and the two of them exited stage left.

I suddenly wished I was the Tin Man, without a heart to break.

Twenty-eight minutes, a giant sundae, and a stomachache later, Yael and I returned to the auditorium to take our seats with the others to hear the cast list. The stomachache was only partly from the ice cream.

Jen and clipboard guy were up onstage. "Hurry up, kids. Let's go," Jen called out, looking toward the back of the room, where people were still filing in. I refused to turn around but noticed that Hiro (and Meg) hadn't come in yet.

"All right, everyone, have a seat so we can get through this. It's been a long day," Jen said.

My insides were churning like the industrial Hobart mixer at the sweet shop.

"For Dorothy: Tara Singh. For the part of—"

She had to stop because I had jumped up and yelled out, "YES!"

"Can we keep the celebrating for the end," she said, giving me a look until I sat down.

I was mortified, but only for one second until Yael grabbed my arm and squeezed it hard. We whisper-chanted together: "Yes, yes, yes!"

"Tin Man will be Kevin Parker. Scarecrow

will be Hiro Nakahara, and Silvio Castardi for the Lion."

I heard my name whispered from across the aisle and looked over to see Hiro grinning at me, giving me two thumbs-up. Was it weird that I was suddenly not as excited to be the Dorothy to his Scarecrow?

Meg was beside him, looking down as Jen continued reading out the list. Then she sighed, and her mouth got all pinched when Jen announced she had gotten the part of Glinda.

I knew Meg would shine as the Good Witch. After all, she was my nemesis because she was a good actor. I caught her eye and smiled encouragingly. I would have been disappointed too if I were in her non-ruby slippers, but I hoped she'd get her spark back soon. I wanted this to be the best show Knot's Valley had ever seen.

Once Jen was done with the list, she reminded us about rehearsals and let us know they would post any updates on the Knot's Valley Little Theater website and then said we were free to go, thanking everyone for coming out.

"It's a quarter to nine; maybe my mom's outside already," Yael said as I stood up. I was about to leave, but then suddenly there was a body in my way.

"Great job!" the body—Hiro—said, holding up a hand for yet another high five. I kept my hands wrapped around my backpack straps, leaving him hanging.

"Thanks. You too," I said, and tried to push past him. "I gotta go."

His face fell, but he didn't move out of my way. "What's wrong?"

I looked up at him, amazed that he could be so clueless. "What's wrong?" I asked, but he just stared blankly at me. "YOU are what's wrong. You only want to be with whoever is in the spotlight. You thought Meg was going to be Dorothy, so you went off with her, but now that I got the part, you want to hang out with me!"

"Uh, well, um . . . ," he stammered, looking at Meg and then back at me.

"*Uh, well, um,*" I mocked. "You will be the perfect Scarecrow, Hiro—because you really don't have a brain. Ugh. Come on, Yael," I said, shouldering Hiro out of our way.

As I stomped down the aisle to the back doors of the theater, I happened to glance up and see Desmond standing near the door that led to the lighting booth. He was smiling and gave me a little wave.

I waved back.

"Mom's not here yet," Yael said as we got out into the lobby. She checked her phone and then announced, "She'll be about ten minutes."

I glanced over my shoulder and saw Hiro coming up behind us. "Let's wait outside."

"It's raining," Yael said, waving a hand toward the front doors. She said it apologetically, obviously getting that I did not want to have to see Hiro again. She knows it's hard to make a big, dramatic exit if you have to see the person again ten seconds later.

Before he got close, I ducked into the bathroom as Yael called after me that she'd look out for her mom.

When I got in there, I pulled out my phone and saw a text from Rohan: How did it go?

I forgot all about the Hiro drama when I remembered the big news.

You are texting the new DOROTHY!

WOW!!!! Congrats!!! he sent back.

Thanks. How's the wedding?

Amazing. Hold on . . .

I figured he must have been putting out some more cookies or something, but then my phone rang. And it was him.

"I AM DOROTHY!!!!!" I yelled into the phone.

"So I hear," the person on the other end said. The person who was definitely *not* Rohan.

"Uh . . . who is this?" I asked in a suddenly very small voice because I had a feeling who it was.

Just then Yael came into the bathroom. "Mom's running late," she announced.

I held up my finger.

"Sitara?" the voice said. "It's Preeti Chandran. Are you there?"

"Yes!" I squeaked, and then had to clear my throat. "I mean, yes, I'm here. I'm sorry I yelled at you, but I thought you were Rohan!"

She was chuckling and then said, "It's fine—I can tell you're excited. I wanted to congratulate you!"

Could she be any nicer?! "Oh . . . thank you so much!"

"You're welcome. I must go back to the party, but I wanted you to know how excited and proud I am. Also, please set aside two tickets for Sanjit and me for opening night."

Wow, seriously? "Are you sure? It's just a local theater."

"Of course."

"Thank you, Preeti!"

After I ended the call, I told Yael what had happened, and we had a big squeal-fest right there in the bathroom. *Preeti Chandran* had taken time away from her wedding to congratulate me and was going to watch *me* perform!

Once we were done with that, knowing Hiro had to be gone by now, we left to go out into the lobby to wait for Yael's mom. I glanced over at the doors back into the theater.

"What is it?" Yael asked.

"Hmm? Oh, nothing, I just . . . I think I forgot something. Stay right here."

Then, without waiting for her to answer, I jogged back into the theater. I opened the door, and my heart sank when I saw it was pitch-dark except for a bit of dim light over the stage—everyone had left.

But the pull of the stage kept me moving toward it. I couldn't help myself and went up the stairs, taking center stage, imagining myself as Dorothy.

"This is it!" I whispered into the silence, imagining all the faces (including Preeti's) looking up at me when I was in full stage makeup and costume, *being* Dorothy.

Then, with a sudden buzz and a loud *kerchunk*, I was flooded by a spotlight. What the—?

I shielded my eyes but couldn't see anything; the lights on me were too bright. Except, I knew who was behind it. A moment later, when he came up on the stage, first in silhouette and then bursting through the spotlight, I smiled when I saw those blue eyes.

"Hi," I said, knowing I should probably come up with something smart, but maybe the light had fried my brain.

"You came back," Des said.

I nodded.

"What for?" he asked, and then looked down at his feet. I couldn't help but think of him as the Cowardly Lion. Although I'd never thought the Cowardly Lion was cute. Until now.

"I . . . I forgot something."

He looked up and lifted an eyebrow, his eyes seeming even bluer in the spotlight than before.

Then, before I could lose my nerve, I grabbed his shirt and planted a kiss right on him. He made a funny noise, so I let him go, suddenly scared that Yael had been wrong and that he didn't like me after all.

He didn't look like he'd hated being kissed. Still, I'd been so wrong about Hiro.

"I'm sorry," I said.

He seemed confused. "For what?"

"Kissing you," I said. "Did you hate it?"

He frowned. "That you kissed me? No. Just surprised. What was that for, anyway?"

"Because you gave me the spotlight."

Desmond smiled and then fluttered his lashes. "But you've always had the power within you. . . ."

I rolled my eyes. "Whatever, Glinda!"

He chuckled and moved in closer, so we were both standing in the center of the circle of light. "You're special, Tara. You *belong* in the spotlight."

"Well," I said, inching a bit closer still. "Since it's here, we may as well make use of it."

He must have found some courage, because just then *he* kissed *me*.

# Going Off Script

"Don't look so nervous," Yael whispered. We were sitting in the audience of the Knot's Valley Little Theater, waiting for me to get called up to do my audition. So far most people had gone, but with every person that went ahead of me, I got more and more freaked out.

Yael had already met with the design crew backstage to make plans, so she'd come to watch auditions. Her mom had driven us and wouldn't be back to pick us up for a while, which meant there was nowhere else for her to be. That was a problem; I looked nervous because I *was* nervous.

Crazily so. And her being there was just making it worse, which was funny because I'd thought I couldn't *get* more nervous.

And then I did.

Because as I sat there, going over everything in my head that I needed to remember (breathing, smiling, projecting my voice without yelling, et cetera, et cetera), Meg got called up to do her audition.

And threw down a gold-standard performance. She was poised and smiling and didn't look like she was going to barf (that would be me) and delivered every line without a stutter or a stumble. If she'd been nervous, it didn't show; she'd just walked onto that stage like the part was already hers. Her singing was even better. How did she get so good?

I wondered if it had to do with her rehearsing with Hiro while I was at the movie with Rohan, but whatever was behind her sudden confidence, I could use some of it myself.

It didn't help that Hiro was basically ignoring me. I glanced over to where he was sitting with Meg, fawning all over her, especially after her insanely good audition, which made me feel sick to my stomach. The way he was acting, I wondered if he did have straw inside his head.

He got called up next, and I watched him do his Scarecrow walk up to the stage, making everyone laugh before he'd even started his lines.

He did well with his short reading, and then it came time for him to sing. The piano player started the intro, and I held my breath as I watched him grin down at the audience, fill his lungs, and open his mouth.

Nothing came out.

Actually, that's not true. Nothing resembling *music* came out. Just squeaks and warbles. He sounded like a dolphin who was trying to yodel, which is to say, not good.

*What's happening?* I glanced over at Yael, who just shrugged and shook her head.

When Hiro's eyes went really wide, and his mouth turned into a grimace, I realized this was not him playing a joke. He cleared his throat and looked at the piano player. "Can . . ." He cleared his throat again, coughed, and then cleared his throat a third time before he said, "Can we try again?"

They did, but this time it was worse, like the yodeling dolphin had an accordion—like, literally an accordion—in its throat.

Hiro opened his mouth again, but before he had a chance to say anything (or squeak anything), the producer spoke from where he sat in the audience.

"Thank you, Hiro. It seems Mother Nature has decided now's a good time for your voice to change. We'll be doing *Beauty and the Beast* in the fall—why don't you come back then?"

"But . . . ," Hiro sputtered, and my heart broke for him right there. Also, it sort of broke for me, because if he wasn't going to be in the show, who would be my Scarecrow?

The producer, who I felt like calling the Tin Man because he obviously had no heart, said, "I'm sorry, but we have a lot of auditions to get through. We look forward to seeing you in the fall. However, if you're interested in a tech crew spot, see Jerry backstage."

And just like that, Hiro's audition was over.

The producer looked at his clipboard and then called out. "Up next: Tara Singh."

*Now?* I had to go on *now*, right after Hiro's audition had imploded? Ugh.

"Break a leg," Yael said, giving my hand a squeeze as I got up from my seat.

"Thanks," I muttered at my best friend as I looked toward Hiro, hoping to get some encouragement from him. But it was like he hadn't heard my name get called as he made his way toward the side door of the theater that led into the hallway, his shoulders slumped, head heavy on his neck. I felt bad for him but realized I needed to shake it off because it was time for me to shine.

I got up to the stage and tried to be confident, channeling my inner Dorothy, the one who wanted to be onstage more than anything she'd *ever* wanted.

I told myself to calm down, breathe, and smile before I began. "Hi, I'm Tara Singh. I go to Knot's Valley Middle School, and I'm here to audition for the part of Dorothy."

"Great," the casting director said. "Why don't we start with the singing."

I nodded and glanced over at the piano player. "'Over the Rainbow,' please," I said.

She nodded at me and began to play. I took another deep breath and began to sing.

I sang my heart out. I knew halfway through the song that I was killing it, and I had honestly never sung so well—not in my mirror at home, or in drama club, or even in the sweet shop while frying samosas.

I was going to be Dorothy. I wanted to celebrate but figured I'd wait at least until I was done with the audition—doing a victory fist pump in the middle of a song probably didn't look very professional.

Still, it took every ounce of professionalism in me to hold the last note and not jump up and down. But somehow I managed it.

"Thanks, Tara," the producer said in his monotone voice, which was deflating, but then I looked at Yael, who was miming applause, making me feel better.

I went on to read with some guy I didn't know and crushed that, too. Well, I stumbled once, but it wasn't a big deal because I recovered quickly and didn't let it affect my confidence. In the end, they thanked me and asked me to take a seat in the audience to wait for the end when they'd be making their decisions.

"You did great!" Yael whispered as I sat next to her.

"Better than Meg, right?" I asked.

She blinked and then said, "Oh, yeah, totally!"

Except she'd paused before she said it. My heart sank. "Yael?"

She screwed up her mouth into a lopsided frown. "It's so hard to say. I mean, what do I know about who sings better than who? I know about complementary colors and the difference between gingham and plaid, Tara, not who has the best voice."

She was trying not to lie to me, but I knew what she was really saying.

*Yael is wrong: I'll be Dorothy; Yael is wrong: I'll be Dorothy*, I chanted in my head as the casting director and the producer left to go discuss the auditions. They said they'd be back in ten minutes to announce the cast. Ten minutes suddenly felt like a really, really long time.

"Hey, Tara," I heard from my left, and for half a second I thought it was Hiro returning. But no, it was Desmond.

"Hi," I said.

He took the seat beside me even though I hadn't invited him to sit with us.

"You did great out there," he said, smiling at me like he really meant it.

It was pretty nice of him to say, but it didn't mean much if Meg had done better. I was going to ask him who *he* thought would get the part but then didn't because I quickly realized I didn't want to know.

"Thanks," I said.

"They wouldn't let me work the spotlight for

auditions," he said, reminding me about that day at drama club.

I tried to give him a smile, but the way he tilted his head at me told me I hadn't been successful. To avoid the awkwardness, I pulled out my phone and noticed a text from Rohan.

Hope everything went well! We're all great here. Your mandala cookies are a hit!

He was trying to make me feel better about bailing on the wedding, but he was just making me feel worse. I couldn't help but think if I'd spent more time rehearsing than making those stupid cookies all week, I'd have beaten out Meg.

Meg, who was on the other side of the theater, gloating like she already had the part. Not that I was looking at her or anything.

I didn't bother responding to Rohan, instead putting my phone away and staring straight ahead at the stage. Everyone around us was chatting, but all I could focus on was if I was going to be Dorothy. Hoping I was. Terrified I wasn't.

Finally, the producer and casting director returned and walked (so slowly!) up to the stage.

"Thanks for waiting, everyone," the woman said. "We'll get right to it. For Dorothy: Meg Hamilton, for Tin Man . . ."

The rest was a blur as Meg did a bunch of fist-pumping and whooping until they had to ask her to keep it down so they could get through the rest of the list.

"Congrats!" Yael said beside me, and I was about to tell her it was no time for mean jokes when I saw that she was giving me a genuine smile.

"What?" I asked, confused.

She did a double take. "You're Glinda. That's good!"

*I guess it's better than Toto,* I thought. "Sure," I said with a shrug.

It was pretty disappointing not getting Dorothy and also losing the role to Meg, of all people, but I guess at least I would be in the play. Once the full cast list was read, they told us we could go and that they'd e-mail us with the rehearsal details.

I stood up and was about to follow Yael out when there was a tap on my shoulder. I turned to look at Desmond. "Uh, so I'm sorry you didn't get Dorothy," he said.

"Thanks."

"But, um . . ." He looked down at his shoes. "You'll always be in my spotlight." Then, before I could even figure out what that meant, he lurched forward and poked me so hard in my left eye that it felt like he'd knocked my eyeball out!

"OW! DESMOND!" I shouted, forcing my eyelid open to make sure he hadn't blinded me (he hadn't). "WHAT ARE YOU DOING?"

He gurgled an apology amid something about a hug and then ran off toward the stage while I stood there, squeezing my watering eye closed.

"I'D BETTER NOT BE BLIND!" I yelled, even though I knew I wasn't. But, ugh, it hurt SO MUCH!

"Poor Des," Yael said, chuckling.

I turned my one uninjured eye at her. "Poor Des?! How about POOR ME?!"

She rolled her (two good) eyes, handed me a tissue, and said, "Come on, Tara. He was just trying to be nice. Don't be so dramatic."

Didn't she know by now I didn't know any other way to be? I pressed the Kleenex against my eyelid to mop up all the tears and followed her toward the doors.

"When are your parents coming?"

She looked at her phone. "Not until nine, and it's only ten after eight now. What should we do?"

"I don't know," I said. "Go online to try to find a new eye?"

She sighed. "Stop moping, Tara. How many

fingers am I holding up?" She held up two fingers in front of my face.

"Seventy-four?"

She rolled her unpoked eyes again, just rubbing it in that both of hers were functioning. "Shut up, you're fine. I'm going to go to the library next door to grab some movies. Coming?"

I didn't have any other options, so I said, "Yeah. I'm just going to stop in the bathroom first. Meet you over there."

After I saw firsthand that my eye was still fully intact, I left the theater to go join Yael at the library. But as I started down the stone stairs, even with only one good eye, I recognized the back of a familiar body, sitting on the second-to-last stair.

"Hiro?" I said.

He looked over his shoulder at me. "Oh, hey, Tara," he said, his tone so sad that instead of the Scarecrow, he reminded me of Eeyore. Which made me wonder if there was a Winnie-the-Pooh musical. And if Eeyore had a love interest.

I sat down beside him on the stairs. "You okay?" I asked.

He shrugged. "Just bummed, I guess."

"I know. I'm sorry you didn't get the part."

"I saw Meg on her way out. Sorry you didn't get Dorothy."

"Thanks," I said. "I did get Glinda, though."

"That's awesome! You'll make the best Glinda," he said, and then suddenly his regular goofy grin was back. Then he winked at me!

"Oh . . . ," I said, feeling suddenly shy, which almost never happened, but Hiro, *my crush*, had just winked at me! Except, he'd been so weird lately, ignoring me and seeming to be into Meg.

"What's wrong?" he said.

I looked up at him. "Oh, nothing, just . . . well, you winked at me, I guess."

He snorted. "You winked at me first, Glinda."

"I did n—oh! Wait. No, I mean, my eye is . . ." I pointed at it. "I got poked in the eye; I didn't mean to wink at you. It was actually a blink. Not a wink. I'm injured."

The smile slid from his face. "Oh. Okay. I'm sorry—I thought . . ."

Gah! So awkward! *Tara, what are you doing?! You're making it worse!*

"Wait, I . . . I liked that you winked at me," I said quickly. "It's just that I thought you liked Meg."

He did a double take. "Meg?"

"Well, yeah. I mean, you've been kind of ignoring me lately."

His face got pink, and he looked down. "I didn't mean to ignore you—it's . . . I don't like Meg," he said. "I guess . . . I didn't really know how to act around you, Tara."

"What?" slipped out of my mouth. "What do you mean?"

He shrugged and then looked up at me. "You're, like, this amazing girl, and I guess I just get nervous around you."

*Hiro* got nervous around *me*? Well, this was twistier than a twister!

"Are you kidding me?" I asked him, because he was an actor, and if he was making this up . . .

His eyebrows went up high, and he shook his head. "No. I . . . I really like you, Tara."

Whoa. "Really?"

He smiled up at me. "Really. Do you like me?"

I swallowed and then nodded at him. Then I winked at him for real. "Yes."

He leaned his shoulder into mine. "Good." And then, before I realized what was happening, it wasn't just our shoulders that were touching, but our hands, too. His warm fingers laced between mine and gave a gentle squeeze.

I was so nervous. Maybe even more nervous than when I'd auditioned, but this was different, like, excited I-think-this-means-I'm-Hiro's-girlfriend nervous. Which was the best kind of nervous.

"So," I said.

"So," he said, squeezing my hand again. "Now what?"

*We ride off in a hot-air balloon together?* I thought but didn't say. "Yael's in the library," I said, pointing over my shoulder to the building next door.

Hiro scrunched up his face. "Boring. I want to do something fun. And maybe eat. Any ideas?"

There was the Dairy Bar beside the library, but then I looked down the street the opposite way and realized we were really close to the hotel where Preeti's wedding was being held. I smiled at Hiro and squeezed *his* hand. "That depends."

He lifted his eyebrows. "On?"

"How do you feel about Bollywood dancing and Indian food?"

His grin turned into a full-on beaming smile. "I feel pretty good about both of those things. What do you have in mind?"

"I have a wedding in mind," I said, and then,

when he visibly leaned away from me, I quickly added, "that my parents are catering at the hotel down the road. It's for Preeti Chandran; she's a—"

I was about to explain who she was when Hiro interrupted me. "Preeti Chandran?" he said, his voice cracking. "*THE* PREETI CHANDRAN, Bollywood superstar?"

Wow, he knew who she was? That was impressive. "The one and only," I said.

"Count me in," he said, standing abruptly and pulling me up to my feet at the same time. "This night is turning around."

I laughed and pulled out my phone. "Let me just tell Yael, so she doesn't think a house fell on me or something."

I finished up the text to my best friend and put my phone away. Hiro held out his elbow toward me, so I gave him a big smile and hooked my arm through his because I knew what came next.

We each stuck out a right foot, and then we began to skip and sing.

"WEEEEEEEEE'RE OFF TO SEE THE WIZARD . . . !"

It was a grand start down our yellow brick road.

Say yes to more
Yes No Maybe So books!

Visit yesnomaybesobooks.com
for activities, excerpts, and more!

YES

NO

MAYBE
SO

What will Yael do?
The choice is YOURS!

*Yael*
AND THE
*Party* OF THE *Year*

TAMSIN LANE